A

POTPOURRI

OF IRISH TALES

A medley of short stories set in Belfast

MARK BAIRD

*This book is dedicated to my wife, Adela
— you have filled my life with joy and happiness.*

*My children Emma, Laura and Adrian
— you have enriched my life beyond bounds.*

*My grandchildren Erin, Lillias, Joseph, Gabriel, Beti, and Teri
— you have provided fun and laughter.*

*And finally, my father, Samuel Milliken Bodel
— your influence has been with me all my life.*

CONTENTS

INTRODUCTION

This small collection of short stories has germinated, flowered, been pulled up at the roots, been replanted, fertilised, cossetted and is now finally on display after a period of thirty years! During that time my family have grown up, found gainful employment, left home, married and now have families of their own. My beautiful wife has encouraged me to compile and publish this list of 'wee stories'. A small number of these stories have a biographical basis, others draw upon life experiences and background, while the remainder are pure figments of my imagination. I must make clear that even with the 'biographical' stories there are fictional elements in them or events that have been exaggerated!

The background to all these stories is a specific time and place – Belfast and the decade commencing in 1960. It is an era that is fading fast from memory, the early part of which, known as the 'pre-Trouble times', was a place where strict Scottish Presbyterianism and indigenous Gaelic Catholic culture permeated one another, but with both sides maintaining a polite but rigid self-imposed apartheid. Then the Troubles exploded at the end of the decade. The people of those times, with their warmth, courage and above all humour, form the characters in all these little tales.

I left Belfast in 1969 but, in truth, I have never really left.

Mark Baird
November, 2022

NAPOLEON'S NOSE

My friend, Victor, was small, ginger-headed and pugnacious. He dominated and bullied all the other kids in the street of the same age, but I quickly learnt the skills of diplomacy, which allowed me to keep on the right side of him. In terms of personality and interests we were diametrically opposites. I was shy, bookish and, as a single child, overprotected by my parents; in contrast, Victor was combative, good with his hands and brought up in a family of three older brothers where the parental attitude was one of benign neglect.

Why the chemistry worked between us I find difficult to analyse even from the mature perspective of half a century on. The relationship was always challenging, as Victor constantly pushed at any boundary which tried to limit his degrees of freedom. On many occasions I would be dragged along reluctantly, as an accomplice, torn between fear of the implications and an equal fervent desire to avoid his scorn and contempt.

In those days, summer holidays seemed to stretch lazily into endless days of sunshine and freedom when we would be decanted into the street immediately after breakfast and largely left to our own devices. With bus fares at only a penny a ride, we had the entire city of Belfast at our disposal and none of the constraints that parents would impose on children nowadays.

One incident from my childhood comes vividly to mind. I was around ten years old and we were hanging about the corner lamppost, a favourite meeting point as it was at the intersection with two other streets. This created an enlarged surface area, oval in shape, which was frequently used for all sorts of impromptu street games. A length of rope was tied to the top of the lamp post and knotted at the bottom to create a makeshift swing which could be used to swing round and round until the length of the rope had wrapped itself fully round the lamp post. Victor, as usual, had commandeered the swing and he was concentrating in building up his speed so that he could do three mid-air rotations before he ran out of rope – a feat that few of us could emulate.

'I saw a great film on the telly last night – Mr. Chips,' said Lawrence.

He was around two years younger than the rest of us and had blue eyes, a blond crew cut and a baby angelic face, which made him a favourite with all the local mothers. We thought he was spoilt rotten but we tolerated him as his parents owned the only television in the street.

'I wish we had a teacher like Mr. Chips,' Lawrence went on, 'instead of auld Da Douglas. I hate him.'

He then gave us a synopsis of the film in which a kind, sensitive teacher had a lasting influence on all his pupils. In the primary school that we all went to in North Belfast, we didn't have such a thing as a sensitive teacher. If you did what you were told you weren't hit. That was the limit of their sensitivity.

'What are we goin' to do today?' demanded Victor, who had stopped swinging and was trying, out of bravado, not to show how dizzy he was.

'How about goin' down to the dam to catch some spricks?' I suggested.

'Naw. We did that on Tuesday and me ma gave me a hidin' for gettin' me sandals soakin,' said Joe. Joe was the fourth one of our group. A thin, lanky, dark-haired boy who, even at that age, had a decidedly pessimistic view on life. He and Victor clashed continually, with Joe coming off second best in any physical confrontation. An uneasy truce prevailed this day.

'I know what we'll do,' said Victor in that pedantic manner which would assure him of a lifetime of future confrontations. 'We'll go up to Napoleon's nose and look at the caves.'

North Belfast backs onto a range of hump-backed hills, one of which, known as Cave Hill, when looked at from a certain angle, seems to have the profile of a face with a large Roman nose. Why that jutting piece of rock was called after the Emperor of France's nose was not something we ever felt the need to investigate.

'That's too far,' protested Lawrence.

Joe and I were silent as the audacity of the suggestion sunk in. Napoleon's Nose was further than we had ever ventured before. It meant a steady climb up through the forest until the treeline ended and then across the top of an empty quarry, before the final climb up to the jutting rock. We were both intrigued and apprehensive in equal measure.

'I know how to get there. I went with Cyril last Easter and it only took us a couple of hours there and back.' Victor pressed his advantage. 'We'll be back easily for tea time.'

'I heard there were mad dogs roamin' in the forest,' ventured Lawrence. We ignored him.

'It looks a long way,' said Joe as we gazed up at the hill which now took on the dimensions of a Himalayan peak.

'It'll be something that we can boast about back in school,' Victor continued. 'No one else in the class has been up there.'

When I look back on it, I think that was the clinching argument for me. I had a crush on Ann Lynch. I had snogged her at Big Joan's birthday party and she had considerately taken her chewing gum out of her mouth. Victor had said that was a sure sign that she fancied me. I now had an image of me recounting our expedition to Napoleon's Nose, suitably embellished, to her rapt attention.

'There's a western on the telly this afternoon,' said Lawrence, playing his ace card. For once it did not work. Joe and I were in.

We set off immediately after threatening Lawrence with all kinds of punishment should he tell anyone, but especially his mother, where we were going. The initial part of the journey was relatively easy as we wandered up through the glen, past old McCreedy's house with the broken front window and the scraggy chickens running wild on the muddy pathway. Soon we were past the furthest point that we'd ever ventured and we were soon climbing up through the forest. The sun flitted in and out of the trees, creating a constant interplay of light and shadow as we gradually fell silent, conscious that we were now entering into unexplored territory.

'What was that?' said Joe, suddenly stopping.

We all turned in the direction that Joe was looking and listened intently. The forest seemed strangely quiet, with the pine trees standing straight and true, like sentries guarding the path as it meandered back down the hill behind us, but every so often there would be a rustling sound or the sound of a twig snapping.

'Bah, it's only the sound of squirrels, this place is full of them,' said Victor, who then proceeded to stride ahead. Joe and I looked at each other and it was clear that we both shared the same mutinous thought but neither of us wanted to break ranks first, so reluctantly we set out after him, although every so often we would glance nervously behind.

Eventually we broke through the forest into an open field and bright sunlight but with a stiff and cool breeze blowing. We could see over the trees to the sprawling city below and we spent several minutes trying to identify various landmarks, the easiest of which was the shipyard with their huge cranes and riggings.

'Let's go,' said Victor. 'It's not much further.'

Now that we were out in the open, we were buoyed up and set off at pace upwards, on a barely visible path, through a field of rough grassland.

Soon we arrived at the base of the jutting piece of rock known as Napoleon's Nose, but now we were too close to make out the famous profile that was obvious from our street. We were elated that we had made it and were sitting on a large flat stone discussing our achievement and the impact on our street cred. Ann Lynch's admiring blue eyes swam into view. But Victor had a further challenge for us.

'Let's climb up to the first cave,' he said. 'It's dead easy. There are steps most of the way up.' And with that he was off again, climbing up the side of the rock.

Joe and I watched him as he steadily mounted the rockface and as he approached the entrance to the cave, he started to work his way, crablike, along the side looking for a better foothold for the last few feet. We watched him as he steadied himself but when he made a lunge for the lip of the cave, there was a sudden shower of rocks and slate, dislodged by his final effort. He had made it safely into the cave but a good part of the rockface had come away leaving a large gap just under the entrance. Victor was now well and truly trapped in the cave.

When I was much older, I learnt a wonderful German word – '*Schadenfreude*', which roughly translates into taking enjoyment from other people's misfortune. Joe and I were absolutely delighted at Victor's predicament, although we disguised it in an apparent show of concern. We urged him to try different routes for descent but when he screwed up his courage to try one of them, we would shout up warnings and advice to be cautious. Eventually we realised that we would have to go and get help. Victor was now a much-diminished figure and I could see from his pale face peering down at us that tears were not far off. However, that did not stop me from getting in a parting shot.

'We have to get you out before dark… before the bats come out of the cave.'

Joe and I ran back down the hill, elated at the prospect of the drama and concern that we were about to create. We wondered what they would do to get Victor down and decided that they would borrow Mr. Harris's long set of ladders and would probably need us to guide them back to the cave.

Victor's father was getting into his car when we ran up to him. He was a combative little man, with red hair and a ruddy complexion, which reflected an over acquaintanceship with the inside of a public house rather than sunshine and fresh air. In truth, he was a grown-up Victor, whose argumentative and abrasive nature was given full reign in his role as a full-time trade union official. He was also known for his short fuse. Far from being concerned when we breathlessly blurted out our story, his face flushed with anger and he threatened all sorts of violence on his son for upsetting his plans for the evening. Then he pondered for a moment and said, almost to himself, 'I'll phone the fire brigade. It's what we're paying our rates for.'

Within the hour everyone in the street had heard about our exploits. Among our friends we never tired of telling our story, embellishing it ever so slightly with each retelling. The precariousness of Victor's position had now taken on a life-or-death dimension and we constantly and, with barely concealed relish, speculated on the difficulty that the firemen were going to have in rescuing him. I was in the middle of expounding on the likelihood that their attempts may have to be deferred until tomorrow when a fire engine with all its blue lights flashing came slowly round the corner and up our street. Sitting up in front, with the driver and wearing a borrowed fireman's helmet, was the redoubtable Victor. It was like the triumphant return of the all-conquering hero. The fire engine stopped by our group and Victor clambered down from the cockpit with all the swagger of a seasoned fireman. He then gave a manly wave to his rescuers and was rewarded with a blast from the fire engine's horn before it smartly moved off.

Naturally, everyone crowded round him wanting to know what had happened. This included Joe and me, both of us conflicted by curiosity and envy and now very conscious that we were yesterday's news. This was not how we imagined it ending. Victor, in stark contrast to how we'd left him, had recovered his old cockiness and was starting to bask in his newfound notoriety. In his version of events the firemen had all sorts of problems getting the ladders in place to get him out. But when they did so, they all cheered and shook his hand and told him he was very brave. Out of the corner of my eye I was conscious of Ann Lynch's blue eyes shining with admiration. 'I think you are very brave too,' she cooed.

REJECTION

Simon James carefully placed his knife and fork in a straight alignment and gently pushed away his plate. He grimaced when he supped his cup of lukewarm tea. The small pokey café, which overlooked the market square, smelt of grease and lemon disinfectant. Many of the windows were starting to steam up but he could still see the driving rain and the grey unremitting skies, which had forced him to forgo his search, and settle for an early lunch.

The middle-aged waitress was suffering from a streaming cold and a small drop hung precariously from the tip of her nose as she gathered in the dishes.

'Will there be anything else?' she asked in a soft Scottish burr.

'A fresh cup of tea would be nice,' smiled Simon. 'I'm in no rush to go out in weather like this.'

'Ach, I don't blame you. The weather has been like this for days now. It's good for trade, mind you, so I shouldn't really complain.'

She swayed off to the back of the kitchen, zigzagging between the tables and chairs with a precision and a flourish that can only come with endless practice. Simon settled back and debated whether he would risk a cigarette but decided against it as there were no ash trays and he could not face the embarrassment of being asked to put it out. The Jesuits were right, he thought grimly, when they said, give me the child before seven and I will give you the man. Twelve years in an orphanage, followed by 5 years in various foster homes, had instilled in him a cowed obedience to any form of authority. Not for him the angry rebel, lashing out at the injustice of his start in life and the harsh loveless discipline of the church orphanage.

'Here you are. Would you like a wee cake with it?' The warm Scottish tones broke into his reverie.

She placed the cup down in front of him, careful not to spill any of it onto the saucer. He noticed with relief that the nose drop was no longer a threat.

'No that's grand, thank you,' Simon said. 'I wonder if you could help me. I'm looking for Downside Nursing Home. Look, I have got the address here.'

Simon held up the letter he'd received from the Salvation Army, carefully concealing the unmistakeable letter heading. The waitress squinted at the folded note and held it at arm's length. He could see now that the tip of her nose and upper lip were red and chafed from repeated attention and the rims of both eyes were bloodshot.

'Clifton Road,' she enunciated slowly, moving the letter slightly backwards and forwards to keep it in focus. 'That's no distance from here, although in this weather you'll not be thinking so. Come out of here and cross over the square heading to the garage in the corner. Continue down the street by the side of the garage for about half a mile and take the second on the left. That will take you into Clifton Road.' She smiled as she handed back the note. 'Are you visiting a friend?'

'An old aunt who I've not seen for years,' Simon replied. 'Hopefully she will still remember me.'

Hopefully she will still remember me, Simon thought bitterly. Over half a century of silence, not a single word or a sign during those years that he had ever intruded into her consciousness; a half-century of loneliness, failed relationships, casual employment, and temporary lodgings. He couldn't really articulate what prompted him, in middle age, to seek out his natural parents; if they were still alive, they would clearly be very old now. The Salvation Army had done the tracing; it had taken months and Simon had all but given up when he received a phone call one morning from a pleasant-sounding lady who called herself 'Officer' Annie.

'We've tracked your mother down. She is living in a nursing home and I'm afraid is not in good health,' she said gently. 'But she has agreed to see you. It has not been easy to arrange, as we've had to go through social services, but provided the meeting is short, at least initially, then they're happy to allow it. I'm afraid that we've found no record of your father.'

Officer Annie had little further to add about his mother other than her age, 79, and the fact that she was widowed and appeared not to have any family. After arranging a date and time for his first meeting and directions to the nursing home, which mercifully was a journey that he could do in a day, Simon thanked her and put the phone down. His mouth was dry and he was trembling. He didn't really expect to track his mother down and now that it had happened, what was he expecting from such a reunion? A joyous welcome with tears shed on both sides? Or would it be a cool and guarded reception with little interest or remorse shown?

Suddenly he had a flashback from his childhood. They were called the Sisters of Mercy. What a joke!! Conclusive evidence, in Simon's eyes, that the Almighty had a sadistic sense of humour as there was little mercy or compassion shown by this religious order, which ran the orphanage. On the contrary, they seemed to relish in meting out physical punishment for the slightest perceived infringement, certain in the knowledge that they were doing God's will, especially in purging the children of any wickedness inherited from their parents.

The orphanage itself was a large Gothic building, situated in its own grounds, miles from the nearest town, with endless, carbolic-smelling corridors and Spartan dormitories, with iron-framed beds, spaced out with mathematical precision. This was the only world that Simon knew, a world of cold, authoritarian discipline, where unquestioned obedience did not spare you from a frequent beating. One incident stood out. He was about eight years old and Sister Todd was reading a story to the class about a family who were going off on holiday. It was the idyllic family unit of countless children's stories. The mother, the father, their children, both a boy and a girl, and, of course, the family dog. The class were all sitting attentively listening when Simon raised his hand.

'Sister Todd, why do we have no mothers and fathers?' he'd asked with all the directness and innocence of childhood.

Sister Todd, who was revered for her discipline and moral certitude, fixed him with a look of barely concealed dislike.

'In your case, Simon, it was because your mother didn't want you.'

The rest of the class had sniggered and to this day, Simon could clearly remember the feelings of hurt, humiliation and confusion that had overwhelmed him. For the rest of his life, he carried the burden of personal rejection around with him like a physical disfigurement, which corroded any relationships that he had. Why did she not want him? What terrible failings did he have for his mother to cast him aside? What was wrong with him? With the maturity that comes with age, Simon could now recognise the gratuitous cruelty that prompted the original remark, and he burned with frustrated anger that he couldn't confront the monster of his childhood. Abuse in the orphanages in those days was not just confined to physical abuse.

Clifton Road was easy to find but the Downside nursing home was less obvious. The road on both sides consisted of large, Victorian residential properties much favoured by the professional middle classes of that era, with their high ceilings, long rambling corridors and never-ending rooms off to the side. Nowadays such properties were either carved up into flats or were dedicated business properties much favoured by the likes of solicitors or estate agents; or they were private nursing residences such as the Downside nursing home. It was difficult to find because the sign was partly obscured by a large unkempt rhododendron bush that drenched Simon afresh as he brushed past it on the way to a chipped and battered front door. Simon pressed the bell button and he could just hear it ringing somewhere in the depths of the house. He was about to press it again when he noticed a shadowy image through the frosted glass of the door. A young orderly appeared wearing a cardigan over his crumpled blue and white uniform.

'Yes. Can I help you?' he asked, his strong Welsh accent giving his voice a singsong quality.

'I've an appointment to see Mrs Malone,' Simon replied.

'Are you the visitor for Mrs Malone?'

'Yes. I'm sorry that I've been delayed by the rain,' replied Simon, taking off his raincoat and hanging it on the clothes stand, momentarily conscious of its shabby threadbare appearance.

'Don't worry, we do not have set visiting times here and Mrs Malone will be pleased to see you I'm sure,' the orderly replied cheerfully. 'You're the second person to visit her this week, which is surprising as I cannot remember when she last had a visitor.'

At that moment Simon was tempted to flee. His heart palpitations were back with a vengeance, his hands were clammy and he felt dizzy and faint. He was about to meet the one person who had been an ever present, but nebulous influence the whole of his life. When he was younger, he used to dream about how she looked, how she dressed, how she lived and sometimes he would create little fantasies that would explain how and why they were parted. Only when he got older and life's knocks took their toll did the disillusionment and bitterness seep into his soul. Now he was about to confront reality.

The old woman in the bed looked more dead than alive. There was a small bedside lamp by her bed. The skin on her face and the backs of her hands looked like crinkled parchment. The orderly approached the bed and gently touched her wrist.

'Now lovely,' he said. 'Here's the man come to see you. Sit you up there like a good girl.'

The old woman struggled to sit up in the bed. She coughed and spat into a metal bowl by her pillow. The orderly wiped her mouth with a clump of toilet paper.

'I'll let you be,' the orderly said. 'If there is anything you want then just push the bell.'

Simon and the old woman were left alone in the bedroom, the silence broken only by the ticking of an old alarm clock and the rustle of the blind as it shivered in the draught from the window.

'Hello,' said Simon. 'Do you know who I am?'

The old woman looked at him impassively, the expression in her eyes almost impossible to discern with her drooping eyelids and sagging lined face.

'You're the bad penny that has come back to haunt me.'

The deadly impact of these words was softened by the hoarse chuckle which followed them. It seemed to convey an unsentimental acknowledgement of her action in giving him up, but also a grudging acceptance that he was now back in her life.

'I suppose that's one way of putting it,' said Simon dryly. 'Did you ever wonder what had happened to me?'

The old woman did not answer immediately but lay quietly with her eyes fixed on some far-off point in her past.

'It would've done no good wondering about either of you,' she finally said. 'What was done was done. I couldn't have supported you both. I could hardly support myself.' Her voice now had a querulously defensive ring to it. She was not going to have any guilt trip dumped on her at this stage of her life.

'You said both of us,' said Simon. 'What happened to my father?'

'I don't know and I don't care,' the old woman replied. 'It was a mistake. A one-off act of passion when I was a little too merry.' She gave a wheezy chuckle at the memory, which degenerated into a fit of coughing. 'He didn't know I was pregnant,' she continued, her voice lower and more subdued so that Simon had to strain to hear her. 'He was a sailor. A big strapping lad, from Newcastle. Probably had a girl in every port. He looked nothing like you,' she added, almost as an afterthought and certainly not meant as a compliment. 'Anyway, I was only nineteen and as naïve as they come. I couldn't go back to my parents, my father would've thrown me out anyway, so the nuns took me in. In return for working me to the bone they gave me food and shelter.'

His mother paused for so long that Simon wondered had she fallen asleep but she was simply lost in her reminiscences.

'When the time came the nuns had already persuaded me to give you up so I didn't even get the chance to hold you or your sister.'

At first Simon thought he had misheard and asked her to repeat it, moving closer to her bed.

'Yeah, you were the youngest by about half an hour and gave both myself and the auld nun a fright.' Again, the wheezy chuckle. 'Nobody picked it up that I was having twins until you stuck yer head out.'

This time there was a prolonged fit of coughing but Simon was so stunned by what he'd just heard that he hardly registered her distress; instead, he sat immobile by her bed, his thoughts in a complete turmoil. Eventually, the coughing petered out but it left his mother exhausted and her voice almost inaudible.

'She turned up for the first time last week, completely out of the blue. I thought she'd told you and that's why you're here.'

'No, I never knew I had a sister,' Simon said, still trying to come to terms with this incredible news.

'Well she looks as if she's done better than you. All fur and jewellery and with an American accent. She was adopted by a couple who brought her up in America. At least I think that's what she said.' His mother was now clearly tired and her voice had an impatient tone.

'What's her name?' asked Simon.

'Shelia… Shelia something. I didn't catch her surname. Sounded foreign.' His mother wriggled in her bed, grimacing, trying to get more comfortable. Clearly, she was getting tired, Simon's time was running out.

'Where is she staying? Does she live here?' Simon asked, trying to keep the urgency out of his voice.

'Naw. She flew over from America. Just to see me. Wanted to know why I gave her up. I told her what I told you. I'd no choice.' With that, his mother opened her eyes wide and looked directly at Simon. There was a defiant glitter in those black eyes. 'Now no more questions. I'm tired.'

Simon paced up and down the small garden outside the nursing home. He drew heavily on his cigarette, his hand trembling as he struggled to collect his thoughts. A sister! Who would've believed it? In recent years he'd become more and more isolated as his itinerant lifestyle did not allow him to cultivate any deep roots of friendship, and days would roll past without him speaking to a fellow human being. Occasionally he would grimly ponder the fact that, if he suddenly died, no one would miss him, least of all mourn him. Now, and completely unexpectedly, he finds that he has a sister, a twin sister, someone of his own flesh and blood who perhaps has her own family… his own nephews and nieces… Simon suddenly brought himself up short; he mustn't get too far ahead of himself, he didn't even know her full name or where she lived. His mother said that she had an

American accent. Had she returned home? Did she leave a forwarding address?

Simon pressed the bell on the reception desk and winced at the loud shrill it made; he could see through the glass window that no one was in the room beyond. Why did all reception areas have this hole in the wall, like a railway ticket office, and the need for visitors and staff to converse through a narrow letterbox aperture in the glass? He was about to press the bell again when the young nurse orderly entered the room. His black-framed glasses had slipped halfway down his nose and he looked flustered and a little irritated. Simon apologised for disturbing him and explained that he was anxious to trace the previous visitor to Mrs Malone. The orderly titled his head back slightly to look through his glasses and gazed at Simon impassively.

'Yes, I remember her, an American lady and very prosperous looking. She'd phoned the day before to say that she was coming, if I remember correctly.'

'Did she leave a forwarding address… you know, in case anything happened to her mother?'

'As far as I know she didn't speak to anyone when she left. And I didn't know that Mary was her mother.' The young orderly paused now and looked at Simon curiously. 'If I'd had known that, then I'd most certainly have asked more questions. Can I ask what your relationship is to Mary?'

Simon hesitated. He hadn't wished to declare his relationship. His mother had shown scant interest in him and Simon had already decided that he wasn't coming back. But it may help in his search for his sister and he could easily give a fictitious forward address for himself, if pressed. Simon relayed the main essentials of his story, feeling somewhat awkward at discussing such a life-changing revelation through a slit in a glass window. But Simon could see that the young orderly's interest was aroused; this was a human-interest story that would play well in the pub to night.

'I scribbled her name down but God knows where,' he said, shuffling through some loose scraps of paper on his desk. 'Ah, here it is. You're in luck. Shelia Schmidt. I remember I had to ask her to spell it. German, I think.' He passed the paper through the glass to Simon.

'That's great, thanks. But can you think of anything else that might help me trace her?' Simon asked.

'I'm afraid not. She arrived by taxi. Local firm. Pete's cabs. They may be able to help.'

Simon once again thanked him and after the usual exchange of pleasantries, including expressions of good luck, and reassurances from Simon that he would be back to see his mother in a few days, he made his way outside where the air seemed intoxicatingly light and fresh after the turbid atmosphere of the home.

It wasn't difficult to find 'Pete's cabs'. There were several of them parked outside a small dingy office with the name, in startling pink letters, on the sides and bonnets of the cars. The office was located on the ground floor of an equally dismal grey building which was largely empty, judging by the 'For Rent' notices that were hanging off the walls on the upstairs windows. Simon pushed the door open with some difficulty as the bottom scraped along the floor. There was a small wooden counter straight ahead and beyond that sat a man in a golf cap and black t-shirt, hunched over a computer screen.

'Good morning,' Simon said brightly. 'I wonder if you could help me?'

'Ah huh,' said the man noncommittedly with his hands still on the keyboard.

'One of your drivers picked up an American lady and delivered her to Downton Nursing Home last Monday. I wonder if you've a record of which hotel you picked her up from. She's my cousin and we got our wires crossed and failed to meet up on that Monday.'

'Sorry, mate. We don't keep that level of detail.' Clearly, he was anxious to get back to his computer and was not interested in prolonging the conversation. Simon felt his heart sinking; the sense of exhilaration of less than an hour ago, a feeling that he may be about to turn over to a new chapter in his life, all of that was ebbing away.

'Oh dear. I really need to try and get in touch with her,' Simon pleaded and in a flash of inspiration, added, 'Her mother has taken a turn for the worse and the home has lost her contact details.'

The man hesitated and when Simon started pleading with him to contact his drivers, he could see this turning into a real pain in the arse. 'Look, if she's an American and has stayed locally, there is only one hotel she would've stayed at, the

Marriott in Hope Street. I'd bet you a pound to a penny she is staying there. All Americans stay there,' the man said with a finality that brokered no further discussion.

'OK, thanks,' replied Simon, less than fully convinced but knowing that he was not going to get any further.

Simon had often wandered past these tall, imposing hotel complexes with their huge glass frontage, and the constant stream of cars and taxis generating a whirlwind of activity from doormen and porters, scurrying around opening car doors and lifting suitcases, as if time was of the utter essence. Yes, he had walked past them but had never been inside one and now, he was screwing up his courage to do just that. As he walked up the rampart to the main entrance, he felt tremendously self-conscious, a pedestrian in a luxury car world, where his shabby raincoat and scruffy shoes must surely cut a suspiciously incongruous figure. But just as he was approaching the glass entrance, a convoy of taxis drew up which prompted a flurry of activity from all the staff around the entrance and allowed Simon to walk through unnoticed and unchallenged. Inside the spacious foyer people were purposely walking about dragging hand luggage behind them, or lounging on the various settees talking or drinking coffee with their friends. Over to the left, Simon noticed a line of receptionists and he made his way over to the one who was not dealing with any customer.

'Good afternoon.' Simon tried to sound business-like and casual. 'I wonder if you could help me. I work for Downton

Abbey Nursing Home and one of your guests, a Ms Shelia Schmidt, is the daughter of one of our elderly patients. She is an American and came over to see her mother especially. Unfortunately, her mother has suddenly taken a turn for the worse and we are trying to contact Ms. Schmidt.'

'Let me see for you.' Her accent was unmistakably East European, an impression further underlined by her high cheekbones and blonde hair, which had been tightly swept back into a bun. Below the counter Simon could hear her tapping on a keyboard.

'I'm sorry, but Ms. Schmidt checked out three days ago.'

'Oh my goodness,' said Simon. 'Did she leave any contact details?' Simon sensed a degree of hesitation and pressed: 'We thought she might be taking a break for a few days to see a friend, but she'll be heartbroken not to be there at the end. The doctor has given her mother only a couple of days left.'

'Well, the only number is a number in the States,' the receptionist said. 'And that is hardly going to be of any use to you.'

'But there might be somebody at the other end who would know where she was or at least could contact her,' Simon responded. He must get this number. It was his only chance to follow up the most epoch-changing revelation of his life; a potential lifeline out of a life of utter loneliness and desolation. 'I'll follow it up if you give me her number.'

'I'm afraid it's against hotel policy to divulge a guest's personal details,' the receptionist said, looking around her a little desperately, hoping to see a more senior manager to palm the request off to. By this time the new arrivals, who had been congregating at the door when Simon arrived, had filtered their way into reception and were forming a noisy queue behind him.

'I'm afraid this number is the only chance of contacting her. Perhaps you could ring the number yourself,' Simon added as an afterthought, judging that she would not, but hoping that it would add credibility to his role as a legitimate employee of the nursing home.

But the receptionist still hesitated. She could see the queue that was forming behind Simon, a few of whom were already muttering impatiently.

'Perhaps if you could come back tomorrow when the manager is back…' Simon felt his chance slipping away from him.

'Look,' he said, 'time is absolutely of the essence here. Ms Schmidt travelled a long way to see her mother. She'll be heartbroken not to be there at the end. Imagine how you'd feel.' The last comment was crudely aimed at stoking the receptionist's sense of empathy with a daughter living far from home.

'Well OK… since it's an emergency,' said the receptionist hesitantly. 'But don't say that I gave you the details,' she added, her face slightly flushed with concern that she had been pushed into divulging the information.

'Thank you… thank you so much… and don't worry, I'll never say a word,' said Simon, gratefully seizing the scrap of paper that was passed across to him.

Simon's heart was singing as he crossed the hotel lobby. He was ecstatic that he had secured the contact number for his sister but he was also delighted with himself on how he'd held his ground and had persevered; so often in the past he'd been overly deferential to any form of authority and would've been easily fobbed off.

*

For possibly the 20th time that evening Simon looked at the scrap of paper; he had already committed the numbers to memory but that didn't stop him from examining them again. There was a number 3 which could be an 8 and a 2 which could be a 7; Simon fretted over the possible confusion but then consoled himself that the worst that could happen would be a wrong number, which could then be easily rectified by trying the alternative. He was now back in his tiny flat and feeling somewhat deflated after the intense drama of the last few days. Not only had he tracked down his natural mother but he'd also received the astounding news that he had a twin sister!

But then a lifetime of hardship and dashed hopes came seeping back into his consciousness like the gathering dusk in a winter's evening. When he coldly reflected on his meeting with his mother, there wasn't a glimmer of regret or even warmth from her; indeed, she had shown scant interest in him, never asked if he was married or had a family, never gave a hint of remorse. His abiding memory from the encounter was at the end, when he stood at her bedroom door to leave, desperately hoping for some final acknowledgement of the momentous nature of his visit, but she was too interested in haranguing the young nurse about the state of her pillows; she never looked round or said goodbye.

Simon got to his feet and wandered into his scullery, a small alcove that contained a two-ring cooker, a sink and a pantry-styled cupboard, which housed his meagre collection of tinned meats, soups and tea bags. Along with his lounge/bedroom and equally tiny bathroom, he enjoyed a degree of privacy and self-sufficiency that he greatly treasured after a life time of cheap lodgings and hostels. His job in the warehouse was regular and non-demanding, and Simon felt that his life had finally settled into a state of modest contentment. However, the recent events had changed all that and the note that he was still clutching in his hand, was at the heart of his troubled spirits. It was now two weeks since he had visited his mother and he had rung the nursing home twice in that period. He used the pretence that he was enquiring after his mother's well-being, but in truth, he wanted to know if his sister had ever rung back; she hadn't.

The question which dominated Simon's waking thoughts was, did his sister now know about him? Surely, she must have done… and if this was the case, would she now be looking for him? In his last telephone call, he impressed upon the young nursing orderly to give her his home address if she called. He was happy to oblige, but said he was now working his notice as it was a 'shambles here' and he didn't know who was taking his place. The more he thought about it the more

Simon realised, that if contact with his sister was to be made, then he would have to make the first move… which meant phoning her. And yet he still delayed! His reasons were not hard to discern. Simon was ashamed of his failure in life. Admittedly he had a poor start, the orphanage and all that, but when he looked back at the opportunities he squandered through lack of personal effort and the relationships that he allowed to slip away through carelessness and lack of commitment, he couldn't help thinking that Sister Todd was right when she declared that he was 'useless and would amount to nothing.' How could he have any sort of relationship with a sister who clearly had a much different life experience to himself and who lived a half world away? He could hardly afford the rail fare to see his mother, never mind a flight to America! Simon sipped his tea and looked down on the numbers again; he knew that he had to phone but was afraid of what the result might be.

Simon quietly descended the stairs onto the hallway. The large rambling house was divided into a number of flats and Simon's flat was on the top floor, in effect the original attic which had been converted and extended. The hallway was gloomy and narrow with a threadbare and dirty carpet, which curled and wrinkled in places; halfway along the hall a push bike leaned against the wall and just before that, a telephone rested on a small shelf. This phone could only be used for outgoing calls and required a phone card for its use. Simon had fully loaded the card in readiness for his transatlantic call and had chosen late Sunday afternoon when the house was generally quiet and would also allow for the time difference. Simon carefully typed in his card code and waited for the signal indicating that he could commence dialling; his hand was shaking and his mouth was dry. He had rehearsed his opening conversation many times but now that the moment had arrived, the negative demons of his past rose to taunt and ridicule him. *Look at you, a silent old bachelor, living on your own, with not two pennies to rub together. A life spent in greyness and shabbiness. A life lived without trace. A life wasted…*

The phone started to ring, remarkably clear and loud for such a long distance. *She is not interested in you. If she were, she would have left a message with the nursing home. She will think that you're after her money…*

The ringing suddenly stopped and a woman's voice, pleasant, soft and with an unmistakeably American accent, said, 'Good morning, Shelia Schmidt speaking.'

How could she have interest in you? You'll be an embarrassment to her. You're going to get your faced slapped… yet again. Another rejection in a lifetime of rejections.

'Hello?' The voice was louder and more urgent.

Simon paused and then gently put the phone back on its cradle.

BUCK ALEC

The name of my street gave the age of the houses as surely as if carbon dating had been used; Crimea Street firmly placed the origin of the houses around the 1860s and they were built to house the influx of people who had flocked to the city to escape the grinding poverty of the countryside. Whatever their expectations of a better life, the reality must surely have been a shock. Each house was identical to the next and based on the simple model of two rooms upstairs and two rooms downstairs with the toilet in the backyard and one single, cold water tap to cater for all needs. At the front of the house, a tiny patch of earth was railed off as if it was precious, and the boundary it delineated, was scrupulously observed.

Our world was confined to endless streets of these terraced houses; their monotonous sameness helped to dull any sense of deprivation. Life was hard and unrelenting, with the ever-present threat of unemployment and destitution, but somehow it never stifled the rollicking, irreverent, energetic vibrancy of the community. The place abounded with characters, all larger than life, but none more so than Buck Alec.

I never knew his proper name as he was known the length and breadth of the neighbourhood as simply Buck Alec. He was a small and pugnacious man, with hair cut so short that you thought he was entirely bald, except when the light caught the silver sheen of his stubble, like moonlight reflecting frost from a paving stone. He had been in the merchant navy most of his life and both of his arms were festooned with tattoos. Most intriguingly, was the head of a snake which occasionally peeped out when the top of his shirt was unbuttoned, and which hinted at a full frontal mural of exotic proportions.

What he lacked for in height he made up for in breadth, and his thick neck and broad shoulders caused the material of his brown leather jacket to strain at the seams. But the riveting feature of his whole persona, the one that dragged your eyes to it despite your fear of giving offense, was the scar on his face. This was no ordinary scar but was a deep red crease which stretched from under his chin, the length of his cheek and ended up under a glass eye which seemed to be frozen in a permanently accusing and angry stare.

It was said that he got the scar and lost his eye in a knife fight with a Chinese cook whom he had accused of cheating in a card game. The Chinese cook had died from his wounds – so the story went – and the whole episode had been hushed up by the ship's captain. Whatever was the truth, Buck Alec kept his own counsel and his brooding and menacing presence certainly discouraged any questions.

He was a man of strict routine who would leave the house at the same time every day to do his chores, leaning heavily on a stick and walking with difficulty, with a pronounced hobble. On a Saturday morning, he would indulge in his only recreation, a visit to the local bookies where he would place bets with a concentrated intensity. It was here that my father struck up a low-key friendship as they swapped opinions and information on the latest races. My father at the evening meal, conscious of the reputation and aura that Buck Alec commanded in the street, would take delight in relating titbits of information, which Buck Alec had let slip about himself. He would precede any divulgence with the same opening announcement: 'Alec,' he deliberately dispensed with the Buck, thus hinting at a closer relationship, 'told me an interesting story today…' and then he would secretly enjoy the way we would pull our chairs closer and give him our rapt attention. I am sure my father embellished the stories that he heard, but even allowing for this, the picture that emerged was of a man who had lived life to the full, in different countries, doing different jobs and experiencing different cultures and characters. I was utterly enthralled by it all and it fired an unspoken ambition in me to break out of my own environment and seek my fortune away from the grey, grinding poverty of my own surroundings.

One day my father sent me to retrieve a hammer that Buck Alec had borrowed. I was reluctant to comply even though my father's stories had gone some way to dispel his sinister image: 'Don't be silly, Tom. What do you think he's going to do to you… slit your throat?' My father gave a cackling laugh. I was the only son and significantly younger than my two sisters and in my father's eyes I was over cossetted by the female members of the family; he felt that he had to toughen me up! It was pouring with rain when I knocked at the door and it seemed like an age before it opened. I nervously explained my mission and must have cut a pathetic figure, standing with the rain dripping of the edge of my school cap.

'You'd better come in,' Buck Alec curtly said, stepping aside. This was an unheard-of privilege and completely unexpected and for a moment I thought about refusing before curiosity got the better of me. It could be my turn to hold court at the family evening meal! Nevertheless, it was a very nervous boy who warily stepped inside. The hallway was shabby and dark with cheap linoleum on the floor and a heavy sea chest partially blocking the way. A strange smell of spices permeated the house as I followed him as he limped his way towards the kitchen at the end of the hallway.

On entering the room, I was so startled by what I saw that I involuntarily stepped back. The tiny kitchen was crowded out with memorabilia from his foreign travels; the floor was covered with the hide of some wild animal, two large Chinese vases flanked either side of the fire, a native sword and shield hung from the wall. But your eyes were quickly drawn to a painting of a native woman in full ceremonial clothes. This was not the picture of an ordinary native woman with her squat broad features; this woman had an imperious air with high cheekbones, a hawk-like Arabian nose and full sensual lips.

Buck Alec caught me staring at the picture and almost inaudibly and certainly not seeking a response, I heard him say, 'So you like my wife?' For a few moments his whole demeanour reflected a great sadness before he turned abruptly away to look for the hammer. I was too young and too intimidated to ask any questions but stood in the tiny room enthralled by the exotic array of souvenirs on display.

When Buck Alec returned with the hammer he caught me gingerly feeling the tip of the spear.

'Would ye want that thrown at ye?' he asked with the hint of a smile, causing a few creases to appear at the side of his good eye.

'I wouldn't,' I replied earnestly. And then emboldened by a sudden sense that this man was not the ogre as portrayed in the street, I asked, 'Did that happen to you?' He did not answer immediately but instead sat down heavily at a small, oilcloth-covered table by the widow and drew out his pipe and proceeded to fill it. This was not your standard pipe but instead had a long ivory stem with a small bowl at the end. His tobacco was a solid hard lump that he cut shards of the end off, and then teased them in his hands until he had thin enough flakes to pack in the bowl, pressing them down with a deeply stained index finger. When he struck the match, the flame leapt and then died back as he drew air through the long stem, his lips popping quietly. All the while, as this small ritual was being enacted, he was silently appraising me with a steady gaze.

'What's your name?' he asked.

'Tom,' I replied.

'Well Tom, I've had many things thrown at me, a knife, a fist, a frying pan and even a lady's parasol, but never a spear.

And if it had been thrown at me, I wouldn't be telling you about it now! No. The man who carried that spear was big, strong and brave and he wouldn't have missed.' This last comment was said quietly as if to himself and again I was conscious of an undercurrent of sadness.

'How long were you in Africa?' I asked, wishing to hear more but Buck Alec was not willing to open up any further, at least not then. Instead, he asked, 'Do you like dogs?' as he pulled himself to his feet by gripping the side of the table.

'Yes,' I replied.

'Ah, but maybe the important question is, do they like you?'

'I'm the only one that Big Ben allows me to pat,' I replied stoutly, referring to a bad-tempered Alsatian that policed the top of the street as if it was its own private fiefdom. Even the postman was known to bribe it with stale buns to be allowed to conduct his business.

'Well let's see how ye get on with Murphy.' And with that challenge, Buck Alec hobbled his way to the small back door and down the steps to the tiny, whitewashed backyard. I followed him slowly, not sure what was going to happen next but once out of the back door, I noticed immediately a large, muscular, brown dog chained to the back wall. The dog immediately got to its feet and stood attentively but silently watching Buck Alec approach it. What struck me was how the dog displayed neither friendliness nor aggression but simply stood there motionless and watchful as if Buck Alec was a stranger and it did not know how to react.

'Meet Murphy the lion hunter,' he said, rubbing the dog gently behind the ears and earning a measure of reassuring response as the dog tilted its head back and narrowed its oddly almond-shaped eyes in a spasm of pleasure.

'Although he has some Mastiff in him, he is mostly a Rhodesian Ridgeback. An African dog,' said Buck Alec by way of explanation. 'See that ridge of stiff hair along its back. That's how you know a Ridgeway,' he said with his hand stroking along a ridge of hair that seemed to be running in the opposite direction to the rest of its coat. 'Come and introduce yourself to him,' he said.

I moved nervously forward and held out my wrists, as my father had shown me, to allow the dog to sniff me in an unthreatening gesture of supplication on my part. Murphy disdainfully ignored me and kept his focus on Buck Alec in the same indemonstrable but wary manner.

'He likes you,' said Buck Alec.

'How do you know?' I replied doubtfully.

'He didn't bite your hand off,' he replied humorously, but hardly reassuringly. He then proceeded to make me an offer, that for every time I took Murphy out for a walk, 'No shorter than one hour, mind,' he would give me sixpence. His leg was 'playing up' and the dog needed exercise. This was a king's ransom to me as my weekly pocket money was only a shilling and he imposed no limit to the number of times that I could take Murphy out in the week. But still I hesitated. Murphy was not any bigger than Big Ben but he was muscular with a broad chest and there was an unpredictable aura of violence about him. Buck Alec noticed my hesitation and said, 'Why don't you get to know him? Come every day after school and I'll let you feed him and in no time, he'll be your best friend.' I was too young to pick up an underlying tone of cynicism that lay behind the last comment.

'OK,' I replied.

And that was what I did. After school I would turn up and feed Murphy either scraps from the butcher's or the remains of Buck Alec's meal mixed in with a tin of dog meat. He certainly wasn't overfed and when he saw me he would start walking restlessly back and forth as far as the lead would allow, rather like the lions at feeding time in the zoo. Buck Alec told me that he got this dog in Africa when he was working on a farm and that the dog had been trained to hunt for big game, including lions. All of this was related to me in short staccato sentences, which did not invite any further interaction on my part, but I was utterly enthralled by it all, especially at the prospect of walking this ferocious dog down the street to the astonishment and envy of my friends.

'There are three commands that Murphy will obey and you must learn them,' said Buck Alec. 'They are in Swahili, an African native language,' he said, by way of explanation. 'The first and most important is "Ima" which means stop. If you use it Murphy will immediately stop whatever he's doing. Watch me,' he commanded.

'Ima,' he snapped. And true enough Murphy immediately stopped gnawing a large bone that had been his meal for the day.

'Ahale,' said Buck Alec and Murphy immediately sat down. 'And the last one is "Iza",' and Murphy came over and stood by him. 'With those three commands you'll be able to control him,' he brusquely said and made his way back into the house.

That evening I greatly enjoyed wallowing in the attention that my account attracted from the rest of the family, although my mother expressed some alarm at the possible danger posed by this unbeknown big dog, my father was more sanguine:

'He'll be all reight. Alec is not a stupid or careless man. And Tom has a way with dogs… like me.' The latter was said light-heartedly, although later in the evening he pulled me aside to warn me to also be careful.

'Show the dog early on who's boss,' he counselled, hardly a helpful comment given the circumstances!

After about a week of ingratiating myself to Murphy which included giving him a couple of rich tea biscuits that I had smuggled out of the house, the big day arrived for me to take him for a walk round the neighbourhood. Buck Alec strapped a heavy leather collar studded with steel caps to Murphy's powerful neck and attached an equally heavy metal lead.

'Well here you are,' he said, giving me the lead. 'He's wearing a choke collar so a sudden jerk with the lead will bring him to heel.' And he demonstrated by pulling abruptly and hard on the lead, jerking Murphy's big head away from sniffing the side of the wall.

'OK,' I said weakly, while thinking that if I did that Murphy may take serious offense! But when we walked down the narrow hallway, Murphy started to strain at the lead as he sensed that freedom from the tiny backyard was soon at hand, and I was forced to administer a few sharp tugs, which I was relieved to see him respond to.

Outside the rain had stopped and the cobblestones glistened in the weak sunlight. I turned right and walked self-consciously up the street with Murphy looping by my side. Across the road I could see Victor MacCallister and some of his friends taking it in turn to swing from a rope that was tied to the top of a lamppost. My heart sank as Victor was the street 'hard man' and seemed to delight in picking on me in that cruel relentless way that childhood bullies can only manage. I was spotted almost immediately and they quickly trooped over to inspect the new addition to the street. Normally, an encounter with Victor was a particularly unpleasant occurrence when he was with his gang, as he delighted in inflicting his humiliation in front of his devoted audience. He was big for his age with tousled carrot-red hair and protruding front teeth; I had never known him without a runny nose and today was no exception.

'What have we got here?' he sneered and then gave a large sniff to re-deposit what was in his nose to his throat, whereupon with a practised hack he spat it out close by my feet. I stopped and Murphy stood rigidly beside me as Victor's friends formed a semi-circle round me.

'This is Buck Alec's dog. It's an African dog and has been trained to hunt lions,' I said in a rush, anxious to placate them but also to move on.

'Tha' dog could hunt f**k all,' said Victor but I noticed he kept his distance and made no attempt to pat Murphy.

'Big Ben will see him off,' piped up Joe Snowball, one of Victor's weasel friends. 'Or Ma Taylor's auld cat.' This was greeted with sniggers all round.

'I better go,' I said and tentatively jerked Murphy's lead and to my relief Murphy obediently fell in to walking beside me. However, I was not to get away so lightly.

'Look, Big Ben is out. Let's see youse walkin' past,' said Victor. My heart lurched in fear, for sure enough the familiar outline of Big Ben, as he stretched across the pavement at the top of the street, was now visible. In normal circumstances this would have been my cue to turn round and walk in the opposite direction but this was not an option with Victor and his cronies watching me with eyes that glistened with mounting excitement for the drama ahead; their behaviour reminded me of the crowd in the Roman Coliseum in the film Ben Hur, when the lion's cage was finally opened to the cowering Christians.

There was a small slope as you walked up our street so that Big Ben, who was lying flat on the pavement with his head on his outstretched paws, would not have initially seen Murphy as I approached. But it didn't last long. Big Ben's head suddenly jerked upright with his ears stiffly erect and twitching. Next instant he had scrambled to his feet with the hair on the back of his neck bristling with outrage and aggression at this intruder and potential challenger to his territory. Murphy on the other hand continued to loop alongside me, giving no outward sign that he had even noticed Big Ben, but I sensed a greater alertness as though he was quietly weighing up the situation. In the meantime, Victor and his gang, who were following me on the other side of the street and had been barracking me up to this point, now fell silent in anticipation of the battle ahead.

I was perhaps ten feet away when Big Ben, who had been barking with increasing intensity and snarling in a way to expose the full extent of his strong canine teeth, darted forwarded in a sudden attack. Fast though he was, Murphy was ready for him and in a lightening move that would have won plaudits in a judo match, had got underneath Big Ben and, with a powerful twist of his shoulders, had upended him and had locked his jaw on to his throat. Big Ben lay on his back, completely still, with his legs motionless in the air in silent surrender to the vice-like grip. It was literally over in seconds, a first-round knockout! I was holding Murphy's lead when it all kicked off which meant that I was suddenly jerked forward into the melee of fur and thrashing dog legs. I was terrified and initially froze when I suddenly remembered the special commands:

'Ima,' I yelled and to my overwhelming relief Murphy let go of Big Ben's throat. 'Iza,' I said with growing confidence and Murphy came over and stood by me, impassive and with an air of disinterestedness that, if anything, only added to his formidable aura; it was as if he had already dismissed the episode as being of no account. Big Ben, in contrast, rolled back over onto his feet and with a fearful look back, slunk round the corner of the house and into the alleyway with his tail, in an abject gesture of surrender, between his legs.

I looked round me and saw in a surge of intense satisfaction, bordering on triumphalism, that Victor and his gang were utterly dumfounded; Victor, in particular, stood there with his mouth agape (he was called the 'goldfish' behind his back) and with a look that reflected bewilderment strongly tinged with apprehension.

'So he could hunt f**k all,' I taunted, suddenly emboldened by my newfound protector. 'Any of youse want to take him on?' Nobody moved or said anything. I jerked the lead and Murphy and I continued to walk up the street, my head held high and my heart singing with joy and relief.

It was a seminal moment in my young life. My street cred went through the roof. The story of Murphy spread like wildfire among the street gang networks and, of course, was embellished with every retelling. From that day onwards, I was no longer subject to harassment and casual bullying, but instead, someone whose friendship was to be coveted, whether I had Murphy with me or not. The fact that I had access to this fantastic beast and could exercise complete control over him, was sufficient to guarantee my acceptance within any of the local gangs and their ever-shifting allegiances.

And thus, my life fell into a very comfortable pattern. I took Murphy out at least 4 times a week, generally for a regal walk round all the streets in my immediate orbit and wherever I went, the kids in the street would stop whatever they were doing and crowd round, with some of the braver ones tentatively stroking Murphy's coat. Naturally, I would make up some outlandish stories about Murphy's time in Africa which would be uncritically accepted and with repetitive telling, I would even start to believe them myself! Murphy, as inscrutable as ever, seemed to enjoy the attention as well and I would be enormously gratified that, whenever I called at Buck Alec's house, Murphy was always eager to come with me. Even Buck Alec noticed it: 'He's your dog now,' he said somewhat sourly one day and my heart soared with pleasure.

My relationship with Buck Alec also improved as time went on; I would do errands for him as well as looking after Murphy and he in turn would become more relaxed and communicative in my presence. I would start his reminiscences off by asking him about one of his African mementos that cluttered his living room.

'How did you come by that spear?' I would ask and that would be the signal for Buck Alec to take me for a walk down his memory lane. And what memories he had!! I wish I could re-live those conversations, as there are many questions that I would now ask that would have delved deeper into Buck Alec's remarkable life. A life that started as a thirteen-year-old cabin boy in a local ferry boat and then progressed through different boats and jobs until he became second mate on a cargo boat that plied its trade down the East Coast of Africa. It was around this time that he got involved in diamond smuggling; one of his deckhands was a native of Mozambique and he had several brothers who worked in the diamond fields. They had devised a system for smuggling the stones out of the diamond fields by sticking them to the roof of their mouths using the sap from a local bush. It was a dangerous undertaking as punishment was brutal and summarily dispensed and it was common for the culprit to be found dead at the bottom of a lift shaft sometime later. But smuggling them out of the mines was one thing, moving them onto a suitable dealer was quite another. The mine owners had ensured, through their monopoly position and blatant intimidation, that they controlled all possible outlets for diamonds within the country. Any attempt to sell the raw stones would, without fail, alert the authorities and the culprit would be identified and dealt with as ruthlessly as if he had been caught red handed in the mine. Quite simply, the stones had to be taken out of the country if they were to be sold and this is where Buck Alec's boat came in.

It was generally at this point in the narrative that Buck Alec would pause and look at me quizzically, with just the hint of amusement in his good eye. 'I think I've said enough on this matter,' he would say and I would then vigorously proclaim my utter trustworthiness on anything he told me. This was, of course, a mighty untruth as I had built up quite an audience, not just with my family, but with all my street followers, and as any best-selling author can testify, there was considerable pressure for 'new material'! Sometimes Buck Alec would pick up the story from where he had left off, but on other occasions, he would branch off into another episode of his life and pulled along with the new adventure, I would be left with the unfinished narrative like a hanging thread.

This happened with his diamond-smuggling adventure. And so a patchwork quilt of his life would be built up, as Buck Alec's reminiscences would take me from seafaring stories, to stories of life in an African sugar plantation.

It was in the latter location that Buck Alec and Murphy were brought together. He was working as foreman on the plantation, the best job of his life, he said, when there was an outbreak of violence from the local Ubur tribe. This was highly unusual as the relationships between the whites and the blacks had been generally good and indeed only the previous month, there had been a large party, sponsored by the white settlers, where everyone mingled and there was lots of eating, drinking and dancing until the following morning. The sudden outbreak of wonton violence came as an inexplicable and chilling shock, although later it emerged that there were external agitators involved. In common with all violent disputes it soon escalated, with each atrocity begetting a more violent response. Buck Alec was clearly measured in his telling of this part of the story in deference to my youthful years but I recall him saying that certain members of the Ubur tribe had carried out unspeakable acts of barbarism on the white women of a neighbouring farm. This lack of detail only inflamed my imagination and sense of outrage, especially when I transferred the events in my mind to my own mother and elder sisters; I was both horrified and fascinated as his account of those far-off events unfolded.

The farmhouse and outbuildings had been surrounded by the rebels and the situation was desperate with the farm owner, his wife, his three sons, several loyal servants and Buck Alec fending off repeated attacks from men armed with guns and others armed with spears and machetes. It was clear that help had to be summonsed as they could not hold out indefinitely and Buck Alec agreed to try and slip through the tight cordon that circled the farmhouse. It was also agreed that Murphy would accompany him. Murphy was just over a year old but was full size and had been trained in the art of big game hunting. This meant that he could move stealthily and quietly through the jungle and indicate noiselessly, with his body language, if he detected wild game ahead. The question was, could he transfer this skill from stalking big game to that of the violent tribesmen? Buck Alec was confident that Murphy would instinctively know that the prey had changed.

Mercifully, there was a crescent moon that night but nonetheless the faint silver light, augmented by the African night sky, was sufficient to illuminate the path ahead for a few metres and Buck Alec and Murphy silently skirted the perimeter of the boundary wall. Buck Alec, who knew the farm and adjoining land intimately, had planned his route in his head and, at 3:00 a.m., was betting on a diminished vigilance by the surrounding tribesmen. As they carefully made their way down one of the lesser-known paths, hemmed in by dense jungle, Murphy suddenly stopped and his whole body tensed in a forward position, staring intently into the darkness ahead. It was a clear signal that there was trouble ahead. Buck Alec had no option but to inch forward along the path as the thick foliage on either side could not have been used without making a considerable racket. Both of them noiselessly crept ahead and eventually Buck Alec made out the shadowy figure of a man leaning against a tree with a rifle propped up by his side. It was impossible in the dark to make out his state of readiness. Was he fully awake with his entire senses alert or was he in a state of drowsiness on the verge of giving in to sleep? What was certain, they both had to get past him and without disturbing him, as one shot would have alerted the whole tribe. At this point he paused in his narrative and I was fearful that this would turn out to be one of his uncompleted stories.

'What did you do?' I asked urgently.

Buck Alec looked at me steadily for several seconds and then passed his forefinger deliberately across his throat. I looked at him saucer eyed and in delighted horror; this story was going to play brilliantly in the street!! After a long nail-biting pause, where I felt that the continuation of the story hung in the balance, he re-started his narrative. It took him almost eight hours of running and walking to get to the nearest location from which he could raise the alarm and then it was a further fifteen hours before a suitable force could be mustered to travel to the beleaguered farm. Alas, it was too late. A smell of burning was noticeable from half a mile away and by the time they arrived, the farmhouse and all the outbuildings were a smoking, charred wreck. The owner and his family and servants had all perished in the fire, preferring to die like that than subject themselves to the savagery of the rebelling tribesmen.

It is tempting to wonder, with the benefit of a more mature perspective, how much of what he told me was true and how much he had made up to amuse himself on the innocent gullibility of a young boy; but then I would remember how he would lose himself in his reminiscences, as he did with the story of the plantation, when he would become oblivious of my presence, and his face, reddened by the firelight, would reflect a great sadness, and then I would know that it was all true.

He spent over twenty years in Africa and most of the memorabilia in his house was from that time. Each individual item seemed to have its own story; the spear was a gift from an African tribal leader for saving the life of his young son from drowning; the African drum, which adorned the side corner of his living room, was acquired from an African witch doctor in exchange for a large, self-wind alarm clock, that would emit a most penetrating shrill at an appointed time, to the obvious delight of its new owner. It was during one of these occasions when Buck Alec was in full flow, linking objects in his kitchen with characters and events in the distant past, that I seized the chance to ask:

'Did you meet your wife during this time in Africa?'

I had been enormously intrigued about his wife, whose portrait looked imperiously down at me when I entered through the kitchen door. I was hoping that my gently placed question would lead to a revelation on how they met, who she was and why they were no longer together. These were questions that my mother had rehearsed with me when we discussed Buck Alec at our evening meal and I knew that any information in this area would be avidly received. Buck Alec took so long in responding that I thought he hadn't heard me or decided to ignore it as an impertinent question from a ten-year-old. Eventually he said, 'I'll tell you one day, but not today.'

Alas, he never did. In an early lesson that life is not a predictable trajectory from the present, my whole world was about to be turned upside down. One evening when I came home from walking Murphy, with my weekly payment jiggling in my pocket, my father asked me to sit down as he had something to tell me. He then proceeded to inform me that next week we would all be moving to a new home. It was located in the outer suburbs, several miles from our present house and would also entail me moving to a different school. My father, seeing my stricken face then said that it wasn't just us who were moving but the whole street as the houses were to be demolished.

'Does that mean all my friends will be moving to the same place?' I asked, near to tears.

'More than likely,' replied my father, but young though I was, I detected a hint of uncertainty, perhaps even of concealment, in his response.

Naturally my mother and father, and to a lesser extent my sisters, were excited by the move. It would be a three-bedroom house with an inside toilet and bathroom and a small garden at the rear. It was the fulfilment of my parents' dream and the days that followed were a whirlwind of activity as we packed up our modest furniture and belongings. In the meantime, I was speaking to all my street friends and the picture that emerged was far from reassuring; some of them were not moving for several weeks, others were still waiting to hear where they were going and those that were moving at the same time as us did not have the same address. But most disturbing of all was the news that Buck Alec had refused the council's offer and was going to do his own thing, but nobody knew what that meant exactly. I raced round to his house.

'Where are you going?' I blurted out without ceremony as Buck Alec let me in.

'Well, I'm not going to any bloody one-bedroom, high-rise flat,' he said. 'They can stuff that. How could Murphy cope stuck in a tiny flat fifty feet up? How could I for that matter?'

'But what are you going to do?' I persisted. 'And will I be able to take Murphy for a walk?'

'I don't know,' said Buck Alec impatiently, obviously irritated by my own self-centred concerns, but then seeing how upset I was, his tone and expression softened.

'I'm sure once we're all settled we can work something out.'

I was not convinced and my look of utter dejection prompted Buck Alec to get up off his chair and limp over to the sideboard, where he extracted a large dog collar. But this wasn't Murphy's usual collar, this one was made of the finest soft leather and the studs gleamed from the soft light from the single light bulb hanging from the kitchen ceiling.

'Take this as a reminder of Murphy. It's his Sunday best collar,' he joked, 'and those aren't metal studs either but are made of silver.' I stared down at it and marvelled at its magnificence; in the same way that a crown bestows an aura of regal importance to a man, it seemed to me that this was a fitting collar for such an imposing dog like Murphy.

As I carried the collar home, with all the reverence that it deserved, I pondered the present predicament. Even with the blind optimism of youth I could see that it was very unlikely that Buck Alec and Murphy were going to end up anywhere near my new abode, even if the council were able to offer somewhere acceptable to the contrary Buck Alec. Then suddenly the solution struck me! It was so obvious that I was amazed that I didn't think of it immediately. Murphy would come and live with us. It was simple! My parents in the past often said that if they had more room, especially a garden, they would love to have a dog. Buck Alec himself said that the dog was more mine than his now and any case I was always conscious of the reserved, almost wary relationship between them. I was sure that Buck Alec would not object. Quite simply, in my mind, it was win-win solution, a 'no-brainer', and with a singing heart I raced back home.

My parents were in the throes of final preparation for our move and the hallway and kitchen were crammed with packing cases of various sizes, which had been borrowed from friends and local shopkeepers; anything that could provide a temporary storage during the transition was requisitioned. My mother, her face flushed by the occasion, was in the kitchen busy wrapping our very limited crockery in newspaper, and my father was in the back yard 'coal house' shovelling the remainder of our coal into sacks. We were leaving nothing behind!

'Hi, Mum. I've just been talkin' to Buck Alec. He says the council will only allocate him a flat. And that's not big enough for him and Murphy.'

'Oh, dear, that's sad,' my mother said absently, clearly not tuned into what I was saying.

'Can we not adopt Murphy?' I ploughed on, getting to the point immediately.

'Adopt who?' My mother lifted her head and looked at me, initially confused. 'What, that big dog? Of course not, Tom. We wouldn't have the room.'

My heart sank with this immediate, peremptory putdown. Clearly this was not going to be easy.

'But we now have a garden. And Murphy stays out the back yard most of the year at Buck Alec's.'

'The dog's too big. And too fierce. I wouldn't be happy with it about the place and with you away at school too.' My mother resumed her wrapping, signalling that the dialogue was at an end. But I wasn't going to give up that easily.

'But Ma, we don't know what the new street is going to be like, who are neighbours are going to be. Murphy will protect us. He's also very obedient once you know the commands to give. Please, Ma!' I could feel the tears of frustration welling behind my eyes. What had seemed to me to be a water-tight case was now floundering in the face of my mother's intransigence.

'Look, Tom, I've no time to think of anything but getting ready for the move. Go out and play.' I knew from her tone and past experience that now was not the time to push my argument; my mother had a quick Irish temper and a relatively low threshold. Tactical retreat was required, but I comforted myself with the thought that maybe there was a hint, from her last response, that she would think again, once the pressure was off.

I wandered into our back yard and found my father leaning against the limestone-washed wall smoking contentedly on his pipe; two bags of coal were lying at his feet.

'How about ye, Tom?' Dad asked, picking up on my crestfallen expression. I then proceeded to tell him about Buck Alec and Murphy and my mother's response.

'Well, son, it is a big thing to ask us to take on a dog like Murphy. There's the cost of feeding him, not to mention worrying about his ferocious reputation. What does Buck Alec think?'

'I haven't asked him yet. I wanted to ask you first but I'm sure he'll agree. After all, he can't properly look after Murphy now, with his leg. As for feeding him, he lives on scraps at the moment plus bones from the butcher which we get for free.' I was now warming to my argument. 'He'll be my companion. You know that none of my friends are moving to the same street. It's all right for Mary and Theresa, all their best friends will be living close by. I've no one.' Immediately I sensed that my last point had hit the target with my father; only the previous evening both my sisters had been talking excitedly how their best friends were moving in only a few doors away and the contrast with my own position could not have been sharper.

'Not to worry,' my mother had said then, 'You'll soon make new friends.' But my unhappiness was plain to see. Now I was suggesting a way in which my sense of loneliness could be mitigated.

'I'll think about it,' said my father and my heart leapt with renewed hope.

The next morning at breakfast my father edged his chair round so that he looked directly at me.

'Your mother and I have discussed the situation about Murphy and this is what we propose. You can ask Buck Alec if he would be happy for us to take the dog for a three-month trial. This would give us a chance to see if the dog can fit in with our family life. It would give Buck Alec some breathing space to get himself settled. But it is important to emphasise to him,' and here my father paused and fixed me with a steady stare, 'that this is a temporary arrangement and that either party, that is us or Buck Alec, can change our minds at the end of three months.' I nodded my head in enthusiastic agreement. 'Now to be clear, Tom,' my father wanted to emphasise the point, 'either we can send Murphy back or Buck Alec can ask for him back. Do you understand?' Again I nodded my head, trying to look appropriately serious and grown up but my heart was singing with joy.

'OK, off to school now and you can see Buck Alec when you finish.'

That day at school seemed endless. The more I looked at the clock, the more the hands seemed to be frozen in place. I rehearsed over and over in my head what I was going to say to Buck Alec and debated if I should omit or gloss over the probationary nature of the arrangement. At long last the end of school bell sounded and I was easily the first out of the school gates, criss-crossing the network of little streets that led to Buck Alec's house.

The instant I arrived at the battered front door I felt that something was wrong. There was no light in the hallway and when I peered in through the downstairs window it was clear that all the furniture was gone.

'Left this morning with not even a goodbye to anybody,' said old Mrs Boyd who was standing in her usual position, arms folded, by the side of her front door, able to monitor all activity up and down the street. 'Good riddance. He was a cantankerous auld git,' which coming from her was a bit rich. 'And he got the NSPCA to take his dog away in a van. Poor dumb animal. It didn't deserve that,' she added meaningfully. I was still struggling with coming to terms with the empty house that the full import of her last comment did not immediately register.

Back home there was so much going on in the house and a great sense of anticipated excitement, that I received scant sympathy. 'Maybe it's for the best,' said my father, the logic for which escaped me.

'Perhaps we can get a dog once we settled into our new house,' said my mother.

But I didn't want just any dog. I wanted Murphy. Didn't they realise how important Murphy was to me? How much I enjoyed the kudos and protection that the big dog provided from the casual street bullying that was rife in our neighbourhood? An image from our last encounter together came to mind with a stab of bitter nostalgia. We had become completely relaxed with each other and Murphy, in an uncharacteristic display of tolerance, had allowed me to stroke him behind his ears, whereupon he had slowly lifted his huge head in pleasure to allow me to finish off with a vigorous rubbing underneath his jaw. I was consumed with despair that I would never see him again and the remaining days in our old abode was spent in silent misery.

But time is a great healer and in the way of callow youth, I was soon caught up with all the changes that were happening: new house, my own bedroom, new school, new friends, so that in a shockingly short time, my memory of my old life with Buck Alec and Murphy soon faded into the background.

*

And that is how it remained for over half a century during which I did my own 'seeing the world', living in different continents, including Buck Alec's stomping ground of Africa; I got married, had a family, settled in London and was now clearing out the attic in readiness for 'downsizing' – the brutal acknowledgement that you are entering the last chapter in your life and have therefore no need for all those empty bedrooms. It was while I was sorting out these long-forgotten keepsakes and relics that I came across it, tucked in the bottom corner of an old wooden sea chest. Murphy's collar! It was incredible that I still had it after all these years. I recognised the sea chest as belonging to my grandfather so my parents had been its custodian for most of the years and it had come into my possession when we cleared my parents' house. The leather was stiffer than I remembered it, probably due to the prolonged exposure to the damp but the studs, after a preliminary wipe with my sleeve, glittered promisingly. As I turned it over in my hands the memories came flooding back; Buck Alec's back kitchen with the portrait of his wife and the perpetual lingering smell of incense; the broad-chested Murphy with the ridge of fur down its back; the stories of his time in Africa. What happened to both of them? Where did they go? Did Buck Alec deliberately arrange for Murphy to be put down as he could no longer look after him? Or did he simply arrange a temporary home for him until he got settled? The memory of that occasion of change and disruption now resonated with my present circumstances and I felt a stab of sympathy and insight into the difficult position that Buck Alec had found himself in all those years ago. Suddenly I had an overwhelming desire to visit my birth city and walk down that old street again. The feeling was more than just simply nostalgia; it was more elemental than that, rather like the homing instinct that causes many animals to return to their place of birth, often to die at the end of their life.

I expected the street and the surrounding district to have changed but I was unprepared for how different it all looked now. If they had not preserved the names of all the old streets, I would not have found it. The whole district had been gentrified; where Fred's betting shop stood there now was a stylish estate agent; Driscoll's greengrocer was now a boutique ladies' dress shop; the old cinema, known locally as the 'ranch' for its predominant preference for showing westerns, was now a coffee shop and a furniture store. As I walked down the street, instead of the closely packed terrace houses of my youth, there were now smart townhouses, double-glazed with hard wood window frames and fashionable front doors. Each house had a parking space at the front, the ultimate prerequisite for the upwardly mobile, professional young couple, and the overall impression created was one of order, neatness and affluence. A far cry indeed from the original Crimea Street.

As I progressed down the street I tried to estimate where our old house was, and then that of Buck Alec. It was not easy but the street did have a bend and a dip in it, exactly as I remembered it, and taking these as my landmarks, I paced out where I thought Buck Alec's house would have been. It was now, of course, a smart townhouse with a black sports car parked outside and a young man diligently polishing the bonnet. He had sandy-coloured hair starting to thin on the top, black Buddy Holly style glasses which magnified his eyes and gave him a startled look, and he was wearing a black tracksuit which was bought when he was clearly a lot thinner. He gave me a cautious nod; I must have appeared a curious figure, an elderly man wandering somewhat aimlessly down the street, pausing every so often to look around me.

'Not a bad day,' he said, 'although it looks like rain now.'

'Yes', I replied. 'Rain is never far away here.' I paused trying to think of something else to say as I wanted to engage him; I wanted to tell him that I lived here once when nobody had a car!

'You've brought up a good shine in that car,' I said.

'Aye, it's not bad,' he conceded. 'Look after yer car and it will look after you. Just like a wife.' He laughed heartedly at his own joke.

'Have you lived here long?' I asked.

'About four years. I bought it just before prices shot up. You won't get one of these houses for under 300K.' He looked at me with his big staring eyes as if expecting a jaw-dropping response from me. 'And they sell like hot cakes. I'm putting this one on the market in the spring. It's too small for us now.'

'I remember this place before these houses were built,' I said.

'Oh yeah. I saw photo of them in the library. A right slum hole it was then. The bog in the back yard and no bathroom. Lots of BO in those days.' He gave a cackling laugh. 'Mind you,' he continued in a slightly sotto voice, 'another reason we're going to move is the type of people who are now moving in. Not our sort and they have enough kids to fill an orphanage.'

By now I had enough of this young man and his narrow horizons and ambitions. 'Well, I better get on. I'm stopping you from making your car a shining example to your neighbours.' The underlying edge to my remark was lost on him as he gave me a cheerful nod as I started to walk away.

Didn't he know that in this street there lived a man who had sailed the seven seas, had been surrounded by murderous natives and escaped, had fought for his life and had the scars to prove it? Didn't he know that in this street there was an African dog of magnificent appearance that was used to hunt wild lions and would patrol these streets like an emperor, contemptuously ignoring everybody unless provoked? Didn't he know that in this street there were people of greater talent, wit and vitality than he could ever aspire to?

I had now passed where I reckoned my old house had been and suddenly, I felt deflated and depressed. There was nothing here for me. I looked up at the heavy black cloud and felt the first drops of rain. A stiff breeze had sprung up and a 'For Sale' notice on an adjoining wall was making a scrunching sound. I turned round and walked quickly out of the street.

AN UNFORGETTABLE DAY

Sean carefully laid the tray down on the bedside table and brought the cup, handle to the fore, over to his wife who was half sitting up, propped up by her pillows and with a dark shawl draped round her shoulders.

'It's piping hot so be careful,' he said. 'I'm running late and I've no time to clear up any accidents.' No sooner had he said it that he regretted it. Muriel was in the advanced stages of MS and the lack of physical strength and dexterity in her hands had sometimes resulted in her dropping things. 'I've a site inspection today and I need to get in and get things organised,' he added in a more mollifying tone.

'You're wedded to your work. It's all you think about and care about.' Her voice was low and matter-of-fact, as if she was past caring. 'You give too much to that job of yours. Not that anyone notices… but me.'

You would notice if I didn't bring in a pay packet, Sean thought, but didn't say it. He needed to get going.

Sean quietly closed the front door behind him and paused to cup his hands as he lit his first cigarette of the day. His cheeks hollowed, stretching the skin over the cheekbones of his lean face, as he sucked deeply on his cigarette and allowed the smoke to trickle out of his nostrils. A damp grey mist hung over the city street, blunting the sharp outline of the small semi-detached houses and their pocket-sized front gardens. Muriel had another bad night and he was exhausted through lack of sleep and the prolonged strain of the last few days. At work, there were rumours of takeovers and redundancies but that didn't entirely explain his current zealousness. In truth, he was using work as a refuge, an escape from watching the cruel erosion of the basic faculties of the woman that he loved, nay worshipped, for the last 30 years. Their daughter Elsa would arrive shortly and she would be followed by a succession of nurses, paramedics and volunteers, that were now an essential feature of their daily life.

He got into his old Renault and eased away from the pavement and into the main road. As he drove past the rows of Victorian terraced houses and tiny shops, a police armoured car came towards him, lopsided, like a damaged cardboard carton. It stopped at the crossroads ahead and five policemen climbed out of its rear, wearing combat jackets, their revolvers cowboy-low on their thighs. Warily they crossed the street and entered a betting shop. Sean suddenly felt overwhelmed by the unrelieved strain and grind of the daily routine; coping with Muriel's illness, the relentless background of violence and the precarious nature of his employment. Nothing ever seemed to change. For Sean, every day was a 'Groundhog Day.' Each one as forgettable as the rest. Today, he thought grimly, would be no different.

With a skill honed by daily practice, Sean swung the car to the right, on full lock, to negotiate the narrow work's entrance and as he passed through the heavy iron gates, he noticed Jason's van parked in the corner. It was difficult not to notice it, as it was painted a bright canary yellow with a red bonnet, silver hubcaps and it had a fine white lace curtain framing the back window. Sean could not resist smiling and felt his spirits lift for the first time this holiday period when he saw Jason approaching the car.

'What about yea, big fellow. Did ye have a good Christmas?'

'You bet I did, me old china. For a start I spent it in good ol' Hackney – not in this Godforsaken place.'

Not for the first time, Sean reflected how Jason's cheerful cockney accent seemed incongruous to his physical appearance of that of a tall, black, athletic, Jamaican with a freshly ironed denim shirt, newly pressed brown trousers and a white silk scarf hardly bigger than a handkerchief around his neck, the total immaculate impression being a testimony to the discipline of his army career. But as Jason often liked to remind Sean, it was possible to celebrate the culture of his Jamaican parents, whilst still remaining British. He had been on a tour of duty with the British army when he met and married a local girl, started a family and had been working with Sean for the last three years.

'Well, you're right to get out of this place,' replied Sean gloomily, his earlier black thoughts resurfacing. He'd not been on any holiday for the last five years and he was living and working in one of the worst areas in the city. 'Anyway, what news from the front?'

'It would seem that we are to be honoured by a visit from the big cheese himself – big Sam Ansley,' said Jason.

'Yer kiddin'. When?'

'Any time today.'

'Christ! You'd think that he'd be too busy now with all his political stuff,' said Sean as he quickly ran through in his mind what needed to be done before the visit. Sam Ansley was well known, both as a politician and a business man - the type of self-made businessman who secretly despised his own employees for not being as successful and as driven as himself. Now that his political profile was on the rise, his arrogance, general impatience and ruthlessness with lesser mortals, was well known within the company.

'Jason, we've got to clear the mess in the office block from the Christmas party and sort out the late deliveries that are blocking the gates. I'll do the stuff at the gates if you can start on the office?'

'No problem,' replied Jason. 'But first I've got to put the kettle on and have a cup of you and me. I've such a Geoff Hurst on me after last night. Are you in the round?'

Sean could not help smiling at how Jason often would pepper his speech with rhyming slang, so much easier on the ears than the harsh, flat vowels of his native city.

'OK but we've got to get a move on.'

As Jason moved off to make the tea, Sean did a quick tour of inspection around the yard. It was a typical builder's yard, rectangular and spacious with the various merchandise… bricks, paving stones, cement, sand, fencing material… all arranged in discrete areas along two sides of the warehouse building. The centre of the yard was clear to allow pickup trucks and lorries to park easily and stock up. The whole compound was enclosed with iron railings with spiky tops, shaped rather like medieval spears, and a set of formidable iron gates, double locked with a heavy chain and padlock. It was a fairly busy place and Big Sam ran a very tight ship so the rumour before Christmas that he was selling up came as a big shock. Any change of ownership never bodes well for the staff in Sean's experience, and the last thing he needed, at his age and with Muriel's poor health, was to be made redundant. Sean continued to wander round the perimeter checking that all was in order, and as he bent down to pick up a discarded bottle, he heard footsteps behind him.

'Put that down,' said a voice, 'and turn round.'

Facing him, a baseball bat in one hand and a revolver in the other was a hooded figure, its head masked in a balaclava helmet with the eyeholes cut wide showing the cheekbones. The intruder wore woollen gloves and a cheap blue denim shirt with metal clip buttons, faded jeans and scruffy running shoes. Behind him, dressed similarly, was another hooded figure also pointing a revolver. He had seen these figures many times on the television, often acting out some pantomime ceremony, which involved firing their guns in the air. Now they were in his yard.

'What do you want?' He heard the fear in his voice.

'UDA. Who else is here?'

'Only another workmate. He's in the office.'

'Let's find him. Put your hands on your head and keep them there.'

Sean thought that Jason reacted with commendable coolness when they all trooped into the office. He seemed to take in the situation with one glance and without pausing asked, 'Everyone for a cuppa?'

'Shut up. Put your hands up and both of you sit in that corner.' The voice was young, flat, male with a strong Belfast accent. The smaller of the two gunmen drew up a chair and sat facing them whilst keeping the gun trained on them at all times.

'We want Ansley. When's he due?' The voice had a quiet menacing tone.

'We don't know. We're just told to stand by. In fact, he may not come at all.' As soon as he spoke Sean regretted his words as they sounded deliberately evasive; what was he doing giving the impression of protecting Big Sam, for f**k's sake!! He felt the gunman's eyes upon him. There was something about this one, a restless tension, which made him seem dangerous. His left leg jiggled in a nervous spasm.

'What have yea got round your neck?' he suddenly said. 'Pull it out.'

For a moment he thought about refusing but realised that would be seriously counterproductive and so he pulled out of his shirt a small cross on a thin golden chain.

'Well… well… well. Look at what we've got here.' The gunman leaned over and yanked the cross off Sean's neck. 'A little popehead. We've got a big blackhead and a little popehead.' He gave a high-pitched giggle at his own sally and then abruptly stopped and jammed the revolver against Sean's temple.

'Ya fenian c**t. I'm goin' to have ye.'

'Volunteer, put up your arms.' The voice of the other gunman rang out sharply. 'We've bigger fish to fry.' The voice sounded older and he carried himself with an air of authority. Slowly the pistol was withdrawn from Sean's temple.

'Right then. Provided you give us no aggro you're not goin' to be hurt.' The older gunman heaved himself up onto a table and carefully laid his gun down by his side. He lit a cigarette and inhaled deeply.

'What's a cockney doin' over here and a black one to boot?' he asked.

'I came over with the Border rifles. Got married and stayed,' replied Jason evenly.

'Border rifles. We bate you in the Services cup final of 1980.'

'You were in the army too?' Jason sounded surprised. Sean on the other hand felt a small glimmer of relief. If Jason was able to establish some sort of rapport then perhaps, they'd all get out unhurt. The gunman did not answer immediately but drew on his cigarette and studied the lit end as the smoke curled out of his uneven stained teeth.

'For a short time. Maggie Thatcher sent me halfway across the world to defend the rights of a few sheep shaggers, while my own community was bein' slaughtered nightly.'

'I was in the Falklands too,' said Jason. 'Saw action at Goose Green. What about yourself?'

Sean looked over at the gunman who moved uneasily on the table.

'They kept us back. In reserve. We were dyin' to get stuck into them.' Sean sensed a hint of defensiveness in the gunman's response.

'Oh!' said Jason. 'What regiment were *you in*?' Sean felt a flicker of alarm at the unmistakably mocking tone in Jason's question and he tried to catch his eye to convey his anxiety. But Jason was sitting with his lean body half slouched in the chair, his long legs spread before him, in a pose of relaxed unconcern, staring steadily at the gunman with a challenging look of amusement tinged with contempt.

'I did my bit,' snapped the gunman, jumping down from the table, 'and I don't need to prove my loyalty to the likes of you.'

'No, that's true,' said Jason evenly, 'but I don't have to murder innocent Catholics to prove my loyalty to the Crown either.'

Both gunmen were on their feet, guns in hand. Sean's heart lurched in fear. How could Jason squander the tiny advantage they had with his shared experience in the army? Not just squandered it but deliberately used it to needle the older gunman with it.

'Innocent Catholics. Not involved in IRA activities,' the gunman sneered, turning to Sean. 'If you're not in the IRA then you're supporting them. You're payin' money to them on the side. Or you're hidin' them. Or hidin' their guns. Or you're votin' for them. Thirty thousand of youse voted Bobby Sands into Westminster... not that he was ever goin' to take his seat. But at least he was a soldier. What I loathe are fenian shites like Ansley. There he is on the box as if butter wouldn't melt in his gob. Pretending to condemn violence, whilst reapin' the political dividend from it. Pretending he values our culture while secretly despisin' it. Pretending to be even handed whilst all the time connivin' with the Free State… and the British Government to shaft us.'

There were specks of saliva around the gunman's mouth and his hand trembled slightly as he held the gun. An uneasy silence fell on the group. Sean at that moment realised that he was almost certain to be murdered. He felt strangely resigned, almost as if it was happening to someone else. Suddenly a telephone rang in the next room, making everyone start.

'We have to answer it,' said Jason. 'They often make calls to check that everything is all right.'

The telephone continued to ring, seemingly more loudly and insistently.

'I'm not bullshitting you. You can listen in on the extension.' Both gunmen looked at each other uncertainly and then the eldest one spoke.

'All right. But one wrong word and I'll blow yer f*****g head off.'

Sean watched through the open door, as Jason crossed into the next room and picked up the phone. The gunman picked up the extension.

'Hello Ann… and a happy new year to you too, darlin'… Mary is doin' very well, thank you… Same here… too much food and drink… OK so he's definitely not coming… OK, all the best.'

Jason put the phone down and looked across at the gunman. 'You heard that. Ansley isn't coming.'

The gunman did not answer but instead waved his gun to indicate that he wanted Jason back into the kitchen.

'What are we goin' to do?' asked the younger gunman. 'We 'ave to waste 'em. At least the fenian.'

Sean looked into the dark and implacable eyes of the older gunman, devoid of any human emotion, weighing up considerations beyond the understanding and humanity of ordinary people, rather like a predatory bird contemplating its prey. All his life, Sean had worked hard, kept his head down and resisted any attempts to be drawn into the 'arms struggle'. Bringing up his family, making ends meet and latterly, looking after Muriel, had consumed all of his time and energy. Now it was all going to end. A perfectly executed, perfectly average, indiscriminate sectarian killing. A bullet in the head, a sordid death and in the context of the level of violence all around him, hardly likely to attract anything more than a cursory mention in the endless tally of violence in the evening news. He looked at the gun, which was rock steady in the terrorist's hand. They say that you do not hear the gun going off...

'Volunteer, prepare to withdraw now,' the older gunman said.

*

Afterwards the police sergeant helped Sean to light his cigarette as his hands were shaking so much. 'Youse are one lucky pair of buggers,' the policeman said. He was in his mid-fifties, silver haired with a ruddy complexion, all of which conveyed an impression of bonhomie, but the tired and watchful blue eyes told a different story.

'We think they were C division from the UDA. They have slaughtered five people this month already.'

Much later, when all the statements were taken, Sean bid an emotional farewell to Jason, both of them bonded to each other for life through their shared experience of one day of supreme terror.

'Don't you be late tomorrow, you've still to clear the office,' said Sean as they briefly embraced.

'Gawd, what a slave driver you are. I think I'll report you to the race discrimination board. What with me bein' black and you bein' Catholic,' replied Jason, laughing, 'they'll have their work cut out for them.'

As Sean made his way home through the evening traffic, he decided not to say anything to Muriel. There was no point in worrying her and the police were going to keep it quiet anyway on account of the intended assassination on Ansley.

'You're late,' Muriel said flatly. 'I suppose you were all discussing the news item.'

'What news item?' Sean asked, alarmed that somehow the media had heard about the incident.

'What! They haven't told you? Well, isn't that typical. And you being such a conscientious wee worker.' There was no mistaking the mocking tone in Muriel's voice. She was sitting up, her face drawn and pale, her voice rasping and breathless, and her dark eyes glittering with anger. 'Ansley was on the television just half an hour ago. He's selling the yard to a property developer. They're going to build houses and flats on the land. There he was, larger than life with his big, fat, smug face trying to make out that he was doing it to help the homeless. All of youse are going to be on the dole.' Sean stood at the end of the bed too dumbfounded to speak.

'Somebody should shoot him,' Muriel added bitterly.

THE FINAL RACE

He certainly was older, his hair grey in parts and he was putting on a little weight around the middle, but Martin recognised him immediately and without any vestige of doubt, despite the thirty years which separated their last encounter. He was glad handing the people at the top table, talking to them, shaking their hands and generally smoothly networking with the movers and shakers of his home town. Martin felt a surge of anger and bitterness as he watched him with his bottle-green uniform pressed to knife-edge perfection, his crisp white shirt, his gleaming black boots but above all, the thin gold braid round the collar of his jacket, which signified his rank.

'Hello, are you still with us?' Doreen's voice broke through his reverie. It had an exasperated edge to it. Their relationship had been strained for some time now and he had agreed to come to this function as a conciliatory gesture, an acknowledgement that they needed to do more things together, to rekindle the flame…

'Sorry, I was miles away.' Immediately Martin knew that was the wrong thing to say.

'You're always miles away, wrapped up in yourself,' she shot back. Her eyes sparkled with anger and the hint of tears. He thought how beautiful she still looked with classical high cheekbones and dark auburn hair. The passage of time had been incredibly gentle to her. A few laughter lines around the eyes and the mouth but otherwise she could easily pass for early forties rather than mid-fifties.

'It's like living with a stranger. We don't talk. We don't go anywhere. And we don't make love anymore…'

She got up abruptly from the table, nosily scraping her chair back before picking up her handbag and heading for the toilet. Martin watched her as she threaded her way between the tables, her lithe figure still able to make heads turn.

He felt desperately sad mixed in with a sense of rising panic. *What is the matter with me? Why am I destroying the most important relationship in my life?* He felt that he was sliding down a slope and was unable to stop himself even though he knew that a precipice awaited him at the bottom.

Martin looked around the room. The dinner function was coming to an end, with people standing around in transitory groups, chatting and laughing before breaking off to form other groups or moving off to the exit. The waitresses were busily moving between the tables, collecting the glasses in one hand and using the other to give the table a perfunctory wipe. Martin felt strangely detached, as if he were watching the milling activity from the other side of a pane of glass.

It must have been the flicker of dark green in the corner of his eye, which made Martin half turn around. He had been working the room and had moved in a wide arc from the top table and was now making his way directly to him. Like most policemen of his age and rank he held himself with military bearing and with an air of authority. He was about two tables away and Martin was awash with conflicting emotions and impaled by indecision – should he confront him? What could he say after all these years? Maybe it was better to let bygones be bygones. Almost as an instinctive reaction to an impending threat he lurched clumsily to his feet. A stabbing pain in his right knee and a general stiffness in the lower back reminded him of what he had become – a middle-aged man, overweight and unfit. But it hadn't always been like that…

*

It was August 1968 and sporadic street violence had broken out in many parts of Belfast between the nationalists and the local police force, the RUC. The university was simmering with unrest and Martin was on his way to a students' union meeting where a debate was to be held on the allegations of police brutality. He was late as he was juggling the competing demands of his studies and his athletic training. The latter was his first love. As far back as he could remember he loved running, winning prizes at all levels and now, he was on the verge of national selection. He loved the sense of freedom that running provided, an unconscious conspiracy of mind and body that allowed this physical outburst like a compressed spring being released.

Like many students at that time, Martin had been drawn into political activism and was a supporter of the People's Democracy Movement. But as he recalled in later years, he could remember nothing of the debate that evening as it was at that students' union meeting, that he first clapped eyes on

Erin McCree. She was standing with a group of fellow students, some of whom Martin knew. They were all arguing about the latest pronouncement from the beleaguered government in that loud and freewheeling way that young students, down through the ages, have scorned the actions of their elders. Martin slipped easily into the group. She stood out and not because she was the only girl in the group. No one would have said that she was beautiful, but to him she was stunningly attractive; her eyes were large and merry, which matched her humour, and she had a loud infectious laugh. She was a medical student, and drank, smoked and cursed like a man. She had small neat features, large, classically Irish blue eyes and long black hair, which she was forever sweeping out of her face. Martin was completely smitten.

At the time she was with another student but a few days later Martin ran into her again at an afternoon music session being held in support of some charity or other. They liked one another and he drove her back to her student accommodation. She invited him in and they discussed feminism and the deteriorating political situation. They laughed a lot and there was a physical ease between them that buzzed with potential.

'So you are a middle distance runner,' she said with a wicked glint in her eyes. 'I hear that they have stupendous staying powers.' Martin's heart started beating harder than it did after a training session!

Within days, he was utterly obsessed with Erin, and it

seemed, she with him. She came from a politically divided family. Her father was a senior civil servant and, though a Catholic, was loyal to the Crown. However, her mother was staunchly nationalist with a long family tradition of resistance against British rule and it would appear that Erin had been strongly influenced by her. This was in contrast to Martin's own background which was Church of Ireland and unswerving loyalty, with his mother hanging a picture of the Queen Mother in the hallway.

'We need a united Ireland with a socialist government,' Erin would announce. 'Only then can we purge Ireland of its past, its sectarianism, its social injustices, its obsession with religion...'

Martin was so besotted with her that he would normally agree with her views, or at least keep his own counsel on them. Soon they were spending all of their time together and his studies started to suffer but more importantly to him, so did his training. They were lying in bed together one morning when he blurted out his concerns.

'I'll have to get back into training,' he said.

'Why? Don't you get enough exercise with me?' Her eyes sparkled with amusement and a hint of challenge.

'It's not the right form of training,' he laughed and stretched out for her. 'I need to start pounding something else... a running track for example.'

'Whatever for? It seems such a pointless thing to do.'

'Well I might just get selected for the Commonwealth Games,' he replied.

'The Commonwealth Games!' she said, her voice heavy with scorn. 'That celebration of British imperialism. Flying their little flags with the Union Jack in the corner as if Britain still ruled the world. I suppose you want to win a medal so that you can kiss the Queen's f*****g knuckles.'

'No, I want to win a medal for me,' Martin replied, somewhat taken aback by her outburst. 'And I will be representing Northern Ireland... not England... or for that matter Southern Ireland.' The last comment slipped out and she pounced on it immediately.

'I knew it. You're a wee fuckin' unionist at heart,' she said triumphantly. 'You're happy to say that you wish to see Catholics getting equal treatment but, in the end, you're not really prepared to do anything about it.'

'How can you say that?' Martin was now properly incensed. 'I have done my fair share of canvassing for the People's Democracy... and I have upset my family and friends in the process.'

'Phish. Canvassing is token politics,' she replied dismissively. 'You need to take your demonstrations to the heart of the establishment. You need to make them sit up and take notice and get the international press to cover your protest.'

'And how do you intend to do that?' he challenged.

'We're going to organise a students' march from Belfast to Derry. We'll be going through some die-hard Protestant constituencies and we expect some aggro. It's going to take us about three days but we expect to get good press coverage for it. Are ye up for it?'

She asked this question so quietly that he almost did not hear it and her blue eyes, with flecks of green in them, held his in a steady gaze. Martin felt that this was a crisis moment in their relationship. She was challenging not only the sincerity of his political commitment but the strength of their relationship and whether it had any future.

'Count me in,' Martin said, not realising that this decision would reverberate for the rest of his life.

Martin and Erin came to an unspoken understanding. He would join the protest on the second day and stay with them until they reached Derry and, in the meantime, Martin would concentrate in getting his training schedule back online. This meant that he would see less of her over the next few weeks, especially as she would be heavily involved in the planning of the march, but if anything, the enforced time apart intensified their relationship.

With renewed vigour and enthusiasm Martin re-started his running program. He knew that his main opponent for selection was Andrew Graham, a tall lanky athlete who came from a well-to-do family in Belfast. He was about two years older and worked in the family business, which Martin suspected gave him lots of spare time for his training. They had competed against each other over the years and the honours were fairly evenly shared. Final selection was likely to depend on the results of an important qualifying race, scheduled to be held the day before he was due to join Erin on her march.

Martin decided that he needed to get away from Belfast to concentrate on his training and he persuaded an old family friend to allow him the use of her cottage down by the mountains of Mourne. It was an isolated spot wedged in between Slieve Meelbeg and Slieve Donnard where the ground was dark and peaty and bounced gently beneath his feet. It was wonderful terrain to run on and the steep climbs on either side of the cottage helped to build Martin's strength and stamina.

One evening he was running across the moors and the fiery sun clouds were chasing over the top of Slieve Donnard. It started to rain, and the sun shining brightly behind him cast a rainbow ahead. It gave him a feeling that he was running into the cradle of the rainbow. He felt a tremendous sense of release and primitive joy as he sprinted onto the beach where the rainbow was lost in the particles of spray thrown up by the breakers as they crashed against the granite rocks. Martin slumped down exhausted on the damp sand, feeling exhilarated and exhausted in equal measure. But he also felt a sense of calmness and confidence returning. He was ready to do battle.

'I haven't seen you for a while. I thought you'd given up competing,' Andrew Graham said as they were changing into their running kit. He faced Martin bare chested, wearing only running shorts. He had a long face, sandy hair and his body was bronzed by the sun. Martin overheard him telling another competitor that he had been training in Spain. He sounded friendly but there was a quiet aggression in his eyes. They looked at Martin as if they were sizing him up.

'I have been working on a new training programme which limits the number of competitive races in a year,' Martin lied.

'Been saving yourself for the big one then?' There was no mistaking the mocking tone in his voice.

'No, the big one will be the Commonwealth Games,' Martin shot back, looking steadily at him.

They lined up at the start and the gun fired. Immediately Andrew went into the lead and Martin stayed some yards back at his shoulder. Gradually he drew ahead so by the end of the first lap a lead of some seven yards had opened up. By the second lap, this had increased to fifteen yards. Martin felt that the pace was too fast and that he would start coming back to him. But he was not slowing down as Martin expected and he realised that if he was going to outsprint him at the end, then he had to abandon his own time schedule.

Martin quickened his stride, trying at the same time to stay relaxed. He won back the first yard and then each succeeding yard until he was back on his shoulder. Andrew must have known that Martin was at his heels because he began to quicken his pace. Just before the last bend Martin flung himself past Andrew and in two strides he was clear with seventy yards to go. From the corner of his eye Martin sensed Andrew responding. He dug deeper and with lungs bursting he finished barely a stride ahead of him in a new Northern Ireland record.

'I hope you're not knackered? I hope there's something left in the tank for me,' Erin said, blue eyes twinkling, as she snuggled closer to Martin in the tent. As planned, he had met up with her, just outside Ballymena, on the second day of their march.

'I'm proud of you. You know that, don't you?' she said, her face suddenly serious for a moment. 'Forget what I said before. Getting selected for the Commonwealth Games is a great achievement. Where is it being held, by the way?'

'Brisbane,' Martin replied.

'God, how fantastic! Australian blue skies and hot sun. What would I give to be there now.'

Outside the rain beat a steady tattoo on the canvas. Inside everything felt damp and cold. Martin pulled her closer to him.

'Let's see what I have got left in the tank.'

The next morning the rain had abated but it was cold and grey, with that fine drizzle that lulled you into thinking that the rain was over. There were about thirty young people in various makeshift tents milling around, some boiling kettles over primus stoves, others packing up in readiness for moving out.

'This is going to be the most dangerous part of the march,' whispered Erin as they folded up the tent. Ballymena was a staunchly Protestant town and home to some of the most notorious and bigoted loyalists in the province. Rumours circulated in the camp that the marchers were to be ambushed by these loyalists' supporters as they entered the town. Everything would depend on their police escort.

'My advice to you is that you reroute your march and not to go through the town.' His voice was quiet but intense and his eyes betrayed the anger below the surface. Sergeant Nelson of the RUC looked not much older than Martin and Erin, had blond cropped hair and exuded an impatient authority. He was in charge of their police protection.

'No, this is a legitimate march and we insist that we go ahead as planned.' Erin's small features were set in a stubborn scowl that Martin knew so well.

'It's not just you lot who will get hurt but my officers too,' Nelson snarled.

'It is your job to protect us and it is our right to march,' Erin snapped back.

Within the hour they formed up on the main road leading into Ballymena, behind a banner inscribed 'We shall overcome' and moved off heading against the flow of traffic. They walked two to three abreast in a single line but with growing trepidation. On both sides the land sloped upwards and as the marchers trudged on Martin had a strong feeling of being hemmed in. He glanced nervously upwards and there standing, silhouetted against the morning sky, was a lone figure. There was something incongruous and threatening about his presence and as Martin continued to watch him, he saw him slowly raise his arm and then suddenly drop it. It was clearly a signal as a long line of young men quickly appeared along the ridgeline on both sides of the road, looking down on the marchers. Martin felt Erin reach for his hand.

'I think there is going to be trouble,' she whispered.

Almost immediately a curtain of bricks and bottles descended on the marchers from all sides. Instinctively they shielded their heads and huddled closer together. They shuffled to a halt, uncertain as to whether to go forward or not. Their assailants started to shout abuse at them and within their own ranks a girl screamed hysterically, which sent a tremor of panic through the group like an electric current. Martin looked up to see what was happening with their police escort. To his anger and amazement, he saw them standing some yards away from them, watching what was happening but making no attempt to intervene. Indeed a few of them seemed to be talking cordially with members of the crowd. Martin turned to speak to Erin when suddenly she toppled against him. He caught her before she hit the ground and he could see blood streaming from her head.

Martin had often heard the expression of a 'moment frozen in time'; this was Martin's moment. As he knelt over her and tried to staunch the blood, which by this time seemed to be pumping from her head wound, he was oblivious to the mayhem around him and the constant barging and shoving of people above him. He could only stare in horror at her small white face and how life seemed to be draining from her. He knew he had to do something quickly.

Martin could see through a break in the crowd their police sergeant, Nelson, talking to some of his men about thirty yards away. He quickly summonsed help from a few of their own group to look after Erin, before he lunged down the road. Looking back on it, he sometimes wondered if that was the fastest he ever sprinted. It was certainly the last time he did so.

He took the mob by surprise. One man, his face convulsed with rage and hatred, tried to grab him but Martin easily brushed him aside. In seconds he had arrived at where the small police group was standing and was confronting Nelson.

'What the f**k are you doing? Why aren't you stopping this?' he shouted into his face.

Nelson turned away from him. 'There are too many of them. I have radioed for help.' His eyes darted nervously about and his face was red and flustered looking.

'But you're doing nothing. My girlfriend is badly hurt down there. We need an ambulance. We need help.'

'You should have done what I told you to do,' he snapped back. 'You brought it on yourselves.' With a contemptuous shrug he started to move away. Martin could not believe how casual and cynical he was to their plight. In a moment of blind rage, he grabbed him by the throat and pushed him back against the police land rover.

'You c**t...' Martin never got a chance to elaborate. His coat and jacket were pulled off his shoulders by two policemen, pinioning his arms. In one deft movement, Nelson took out his truncheon and smashed it at full force against his kneecap. Immediately Martin was engulfed in a pain so intense that it seemed to take over his entire being. The rest was a red blur in which he slipped in and out of consciousness. Vaguely he remembered being thrown into a police Land Rover before he passed out completely.

*

The policeman was now moving through the tables, skirting

round the various empty chairs, which the departing audience had left scattered across the floor. He held himself erect, his hair now silvery but he looked smaller and slighter than Martin remembered. He stopped to shake hands with various people and it struck Martin that he did so awkwardly until he realised that he was doing so with his left hand as his right arm lay inertly by his side. He was almost level with Martin's table when he suddenly swung round in response to his name being called. A middle-aged woman with platinum blonde hair and a heavily made-up face, which reminded Martin of brittle porcelain, greeted him in an animated manner. Martin stood uncertainly against the table, moving his feet to redistribute his weight away from his aching joints. He felt his resolution draining away. *This is stupid,* he thought. *He is never going to remember the episode and anyway what can he say or do about it now?* Martin turned round to re-find his seat when all of a sudden, the memories came flooding back again.

Fellow students came to see him in hospital to gently break the news that Erin's head wound had led to internal bleeding and that she'd never regained consciousness. It appears naïve, in retrospect, to recall their outraged certainty that her death would result in a huge public outcry and would lead to major political changes. None of them realised then, the long Cavalry that was ahead for Northern Ireland, and that Erin's death would soon be lost in a blizzard of atrocities. Then there were the numerous operations to repair the shattered knee and the final meeting with the surgeon who told him breezily that this was the best that it was going to get. He abandoned his studies and for years was lost to depression. Then came the nightmares, the flashbacks, the failing marriage and the lack of closure… No, he could not just allow this moment to pass.

'Excuse me,' Martin said. Close up, he was startled to see a scar that ran from his left eye, the full length of his face and underneath his chin. His right eye had that motionless frozen stare of the false eye and time and responsibilities had carved their marks on Nelson's brow and the side of his mouth.

'Yes?' His tone was friendly but Martin sensed a certain wariness.

'I don't suppose you remember me or the student march I was on a way back in 1968?'

'There were many marches around that time.' Nelson was now fully alert and was looking at Martin attentively.

'A young student girl was killed by a brick thrown by a mob. A mob that you did nothing to control.' Martin felt himself starting to shake with the pent-up emotion of years.

'Was this outside Ballymena?' Nelson asked quietly.

'Yes. I'm glad to see that you do remember. You might also remember the young male student who came to you for help. You smashed his knee with your baton.'

'And that was you?' It was more of a statement than a question.

'One life destroyed and one life ruined.' Martin felt tears welling up. Tears for a lost youth; tears for Erin; tears for what might have been. Nelson reached out and touched his arm.

'What happened that day in Ballymena was wrong and as the officer in charge and the officer who struck you that day, I am sorry. Deeply and genuinely sorry.' Martin looked at him. He was expecting him to add the usual caveats: 'But you have to understand…' or, 'We did what we thought was best…' But he did not try to qualify or seek excuses for his actions that day. Instead, his whole demeanour reflected a tired sadness and a compassion that struck Martin forcibly.

'We are all victims of this conflict,' he said and with a polite nod Nelson continued towards the exit.

'You look as if you have seen a ghost. What's the matter with you now?' Doreen may have sounded irritated but her eyes betrayed her concern. Martin had been standing as if rooted to the spot. He was deathly white and was leaning on the table with one hand. He turned and looked at her and suddenly he felt a surge of relief and joy as if some malignant demon had at last been banished. He felt all the pent-up bitterness draining away, and he was left feeling exhausted but also, somehow, elated. He saw with a vivid clarity that everyone, in his or her different ways, had been damaged by this monstrous conflict. The policeman was right everyone was a victim.

'No, I'm fine,' he said and then added, 'And everything is going to be all right now.' He reached out and hugged her tightly to him.

THE REUNION

Earnest Saunders carefully examined his face in the bathroom mirror. Even his mother never thought he was handsome, but the years had chiselled away at his features, so that the thick lips and busy eyebrows were now complemented by the greying temples and the deep lines etched into his cheeks and the edge of his mouth. He splashed on some aftershave, momentarily savouring the stinging sensation on his skin and the sharp expensive smell before turning suddenly and leaving the bathroom. He was below average height but was well built with broad shoulders and all his movements had a decisive, pent-up energy about them. In the bedroom his suit was carefully laid out on the bed and a crisp white shirt hung on a rail of the walk-in wardrobe. He dressed quickly, fitting his solid gold cufflinks and Hermès silk red tie whilst reflecting on the forthcoming evening. He was determined to look his best because, almost subliminally, he had been waiting for this night for the last twenty-five years. His great regret was that Shelia was not there to enjoy it with him. She had passed away just over two years ago with breast cancer and his life had lost its colour and zest. He had buried himself in work, seeking solace and distraction in the cut and thrust of business life, but it did not disguise the sense of emptiness that he felt. He took a final look in the mirror and made a quick adjustment of his tie. He would take the Bentley coupé for the night. After all, he wanted to impress.

Simon Caulfield slipped into the front seat and automatically reached out to adjust the rear-view mirror. Although the car was nearly eight years old, he still relished the smell of expensive leather and its deep-throated roar when the ignition was turned on. A black Porsche 932 GTI could still make the discerning motorist turn and stare and Simon was a man much given to outward displays of status. Tall and athletically built with a lean face, tanned to a dark brown, and clear blue eye; he was dressed immaculately in a dark blazer with a blue shirt opened at the neck. Simon had, until recently, lived in the Far East and Dubai, but his relationships with the relatively small British community out there had soured and the social shutters had closed down on him. Tonight, was an opportunity for him to network. Not a great opportunity, he thought grimly, but ever since he had returned to his home town, he'd found it difficult to break into any social circle; mainly through his own casual neglect, he'd lost contact with all of his old friends.

Barbara Morris nervously fingered her necklace and glanced round the room for the umpteenth time. She was a tall woman with dark auburn hair who held herself erect, which gave her a slightly regal appearance. Everything looked in place, the tables were positioned at the far end of the hall, wine glasses and beer glasses were arranged in regimented rows, sparkling under the harsh lights, and a crisp white tablecloth covered the plates of snacks that her small band of volunteers had prepared. Around the walls of the church hall, there were little clumps of balloons striving to give a festive air to the occasion, but looking rather forlorn, and at the back of the hall a large banner proclaimed 'Welcome to the class of 1982'. This was the culmination of several months' planning but from this point on she would have no control. How many would turn up and how well the evening would go is one of the great imponderables with any school reunion, especially one that is celebrating a twenty-fifth reunion. She vowed never to do it again; for one thing tracking everyone down had been a nightmare.

'Did I tell you I ran into Simon Caulfield last week?' Joan's shrill voice broke into her reverie. Joan Simmons was the classroom gossip and the maturity of middle age had not dimmed her natural nosiness or capacity for causing mischief; on the contrary, her skills seemed to have been honed by experience. Now she was at Barbara's elbow looking up at her with her small black eyes, sharply watching for any reaction.

'Simon! No!! Where did you see him?' Almost immediately Barbara regretted her startled reaction and felt her face flushing under Joan's steady gaze. *The little cow*, thought Barbara. She knew perfectly well that they'd been an item during their final year at school and that Simon had dumped her in the last weeks of term, which caused her to do disappointingly badly in her final exams. But what no one else knew was that she'd thought she was pregnant as well during those vital weeks. How well she remembered her feelings of desperation, verging on panic and her sense of isolation and shame with no one to confide in. Barbara had always kept herself slightly apart from her school friends; to some it came across as superior, and her fall from grace, if it had got out, would have been sensational. She even resisted telling Simon, although that was partly due to her sense of bitterness towards him at the casual way he'd finished the relationship. At least the relief at discovering that she wasn't pregnant went some way towards mitigating her upset over her exam performance. Instead of Oxford, as had been widely expected, she ended up going to Sheffield to do sociology. Her mother had been so disappointed that not once did she visit Barbara in Sheffield or ask her about her course; even when she graduated, she contrived to have the 'flu to avoid attending the ceremony.

'I ran into him at Marks and Spencer's in town. I told him about this evening and he said that he would come if he was free,' replied Joan. 'I have to say that he looks even dishier than when we knew him.' Joan's little black eyes glittered with barely contained delight.

'Well, it'll be no great loss if he doesn't,' Barbara said brusquely and moved off to greet some new arrivals who were coming through the door. But her heart was thumping with the news. Simon had been her first great love and time had long ago washed away the angst of those early times; indeed, many times over the years, she'd wondered where he was, what he was doing and more importantly, if he ever got married. She had married Nigel Morris who'd been two years ahead of her at school, a solid and worthy member of the comfortable middle classes whom her mother heartily approved of, but who Barbara now found suffocatingly boring. She now believed that she'd married Nigel as an act of atonement to her mother, but whatever the subliminal reason, the marriage was over in all but in name and there was tacit agreement between them that they would go their separate ways.

'Hi. I'm Jim Davidson. I was in your class for French,' the new arrival added helpfully.

'Of course,' Barbara replied but she still struggled to link the small, fat, middle-aged man with her recollection of anyone in her class group.

'Were you also in my…'

She was about to prod further when she noticed him standing near the entrance. She would have recognised him immediately even if Joan had not pre-warned her. He was casually leaning against the wall talking to someone that Barbara didn't recognise, looking lean, tanned and fit; my God, Joan was right, he had improved with age!

Earnest Saunders quietly prowled around the room, stopping from time to time to speak to specific individuals or to join in small groups. In almost all cases, no one recognised him immediately and he relished the look of surprise and curiosity in their eyes when he introduced himself. He was deliberately circumspect when they quizzed him on what he was currently doing. He wanted to keep the speculation going for a little longer and then choose the moment for revelation.

Looking around, Earnest noticed a tall woman by the door, who looked vaguely familiar, standing talking to a small rotund man and a tall well-dressed man. He looked again at the tall man and suddenly realised that he was looking at the tormentor of his youth.

Simon Caulfield had it all in those days: good looks, good at sports, enough charm to deflect the teachers' anger over his lazy attitude to work and of course, his undeniable popularity with all the girls in the class. He also had a vicious tongue which he used relentlessly on Earnest, mocking his poor academic and sporting prowess and calling him the 'fastest schoolboy in West High school', a cruel parody of a popular song at the time. But more hurtfully he played on the fact that Earnest, who had a slightly swarthy complexion (attributed to a distant Spanish ancestor) and a school blazer patched at the elbows and frayed at the cuffs, did not wash regularly and smelt as a consequence. Whenever Simon saw him in the corridor he would hold his nose, turn round to his group of admiring acolytes and declare loudly that there was a dangerous substance approaching and for everyone to don their gas masks. That would be the signal for the group to cup both hands over their noses and mouths and to emit choking sounds as they passed. It is no wonder that Earnest hated school and left as early as he could without doing any of the university entrance exams. But as he looked across at the elegant figure of Simon Caulfield, leaning with casual arrogance against the wall, Earnest felt that tonight could be his chance for retribution.

With a practiced eye Simon surveyed the crowd that had already arrived in the hall and who were standing about in small groups talking with the somewhat forced animation that people with little in common other than an early acquaintanceship, were inclined to do. With an inward groan he wished that he hadn't come; they all looked to be the 'petty bourgeoisie' that lived lives of insular ease within the lower ranks of the professional classes. But with a sigh he resolved to make the best of it and who knows what might turn up? He had noticed a beautifully sleek Bentley car parked outside but then dismissed it as likely to belong to a patron of the adjoining pub. Suddenly he noticed her standing near the back and talking to a small fat man with receding black hair. *Well, well.* He had idly wondered if she would be here tonight and here she was, broader in the beam than when he knew her, but still a good-looking woman.

'Hi, Barbara, how are you doing? You haven't changed a bit and you look wonderful.' Simon flashed his winning smile and was amused at her flustered reaction as she wrestled with her conflicted desire to give him a cool response, with that of an uncontrolled rekindling of sexual attraction.

'Oh, hi, Simon. Joan said that you were back in town and might honour us with your presence,' Barbara replied, determined to regain her poise although conscious that her neck was starting to flush. 'I believe that you've been working abroad?'

'Yep. You name a country in the Far East and I've worked there. Hong Kong, Singapore, China, Thailand. I've worked in all of them but now I've decided to lay down the white man's burden and spend some time back home,' Simon said, with a slight dismissive gesture of his hand.

'Are you here on holiday or permanently?' Barbara asked.

'Nothing is for permanent, dear,' Simon said, locking his eyes onto Barbara who looked away, embarrassed at the blatant come-on. Older women were not usually on his menu, but she might be useful and he could sense that she was intrigued by him despite the outward show of careful indifference. 'No, I'm here to see what business opportunities may be around.'

'Well, you won't find much here,' Barbara said, turning slightly to look round the room, unsure how best to respond to Simon. At that moment she noticed a well-dressed and stocky man making a beeline to both of them.

'Hello. Simon Caulfield, I presume.' Earnest addressed Simon directly and enjoyed the look of puzzlement in his eyes. 'I'm Earnest Saunders.'

He had his eyes firmly on Simon. He could see that he looked both uncomfortable and wary.

'Hi. How have you been?' replied Simon noncommittedly.

'I've been doing just fine. And how about you?'

There was an aggressive directness in Earnest's question that caught Simon off guard.

'Well, I've been working abroad for the last twenty years. Mainly in the Far East.'

'And what made you return to these grey shores?' Earnest asked.

'Certainly not the weather,' Simon replied, shortly. He was annoyed at this unexpected interruption, especially when he felt that he was getting some traction with his ex-girlfriend; and who would have thought that this little tyke, Earnest Saunders, would turn up tonight?

Barbara who felt a little cut out of the conversation, intervened, 'Hi, Earnest, nice to see you. I'm Barbara Morris, previously Galway. We're just discussing how depressed this area is now. My husband was telling me that even Mackies is in trouble financially.' In fact, her husband talked about little else as his company was a main supplier of parts to Mackies. 'The company is such a big employer in this town that the whole area would be devastated if it closed.' Barbara felt a spasm of anxiety as she spoke. Nigel rarely spoke about his business but recently he'd sat down with her and explained the potential impact of such a closure to their lifestyle; the house, the cars, the apartment in the South of France and worse of all, her beloved horses.

'Every business failure brings with it opportunities. There would be good pickings in some parts of the business. I would break it up and sell off the profitable parts.' There was a lofty, almost condescending edge to Simon's voice. After all, this was the world-weary, experienced businessman talking to the schoolteacher and the former school oink.

'But that would ignore any long-term potential,' Earnest said quietly.

'Naw,' replied Simon dismissively and then warming to his theme. 'I've been involved in a number of these ventures.

When a business is about to go tits up it's important to get in there quickly. Stop all activities. Gut the assets. Sell quickly and get out. Trying to make a go of Mackies would be a dumb thing to do.'

'I may have been dumb at school but I am not dumb in business. I've just bought Mackies,' Earnest said.

Looking back, Earnest would regard that moment as the cathartic moment in his life. He felt that he had purged himself of the humiliations and crushing sense of inferiority that had been his legacy from school. His announcement had been electrifying and before the end of the evening had gone round everyone in the hall. He had particularly enjoyed the way in which Simon had tried to backpedal and ingratiate himself to him. It didn't take Earnest long to sus out that Simon was in fact on his uppers and desperately seeking a job. He watched, with a certain amused contempt, the thin line of perspiration on Simon's upper lip as he extolled his business experiences and triumphs in the Far East. He was certainly putting it out, thought Earnest, and suddenly an idea struck him. He needed a 'gofer', someone who would chase up all the loose ends associated with the purchase of Mackies. Caulfield could fit the bill. He would use him, drive him hard, put him through some humiliating hoops and all the while hold out the prospect of a senior position, maybe CEO, when the firm was finally up and running. Then he would have a 'much regrettable' eyeball interview with Simon, where he would thank him for his hard work, but would say, that after careful reflection he felt that they were not a good fit.

He would cite differences in attitude and personality and would refer back to their time at school when those differences were most pronounced. Simon would be under no illusion, that whatever was now being said, whatever sugar coating that was being applied, this was payback time.

'We must talk some more, Simon. Have you a card?' Earnest asked and was secretly delighted at the haste and abject gratitude Simon displayed as he rummaged through his wallet.

And if that was not enough for a perfect evening, Earnest capped it by giving Barbara a lift back home. He'd always fancied her at school but from afar, as he believed that she was way out of his league. But now she was delighted to come out for dinner to discuss how they could expand the past pupils' association. And she also said how much she loved the Bentley!

ABSOLUTION

When his father died Liam was too young to remember him. His mother tried to keep his memory alive, but even here, the conversations she had with him only created a mosaic of fragmentary incidents centred round moments of happiness in their short-married life. Basic information such as where his father was born, his early life, whether he had any siblings, how they met, all this was missing from the picture. These questions would for ever remain unanswered now that his mother had died too.

Liam roughly wiped at the condensation and peered despondently out of the window. The rain needled out of a grey sky, creating a thin curtain of mist further out to sea that obliterated the outline of the Skerry Islands, a bare crop of rocks, home to thousands of squawking seagulls. Their cottage was the last one leading out of the village along the coastal road. It was built in the traditional style of a fisherman's cottage with local dark stone, a low slate roof and small windows; cosy looking from the outside but dark and claustrophobic from the inside. It was set some distance apart from their nearest neighbour and that added privacy was greatly prized by Liam's stepfather. He worked as a casual labourer on the fishing boats, sometimes as a deckhand where he could be at sea for several days, but more recently, ashore doing odd jobs unloading the catch.

The sound of footsteps on the gravel path outside the door brought Liam out of his reverie. He looked up to see his stepfather framing the door way. The bright daylight behind him made Liam squint as he tried to make out the expression on his face. The effort wasn't necessary.

'Haven't ye peeled those spuds yet? Ye lazy wee shite.' Donal Meade kicked off his boots, sending a spray of mud across the linoleum-covered floor. He was a strongly built, thickset man, with a long lugubrious face and small deep-set eyes. Those eyes glittered with dislike as he looked over at Liam hunched over the basin, peeling the potatoes. 'Yer mother spoilt you. I told her ye needed hardening up. Lying around readin' books all day.'

Well, there's no chance of you doing that, Liam thought quietly. *You'd have to be able to read first.* But he kept his counsel. Liam was nearly sixteen but big for his age and he felt time was on his side, especially as his stepfather was drinking heavily and his health had noticeably deteriorated, especially since his mother's death.

'And you can clean these out for our dinner,' Meade snarled as he slammed two trout onto the draining board. Liam looked at the two dead fish lying wet and glistening on the table with their dead eyes looking coldly upwards. He hated doing this, hated the feel of the wet slippery skin, the way that their entrails tumbled out when he sliced their underbelly, but he was determined not to flinch as his stepfather would see it as a weakness.

Liam had left school last week even though he was urged to stay on by his headmaster.

'Liam, you have the ability to get a scholarship into university. Don't throw it all up. Please think about it.'

Good old 'stormy weathers'. Mr. Weatherall, the headmaster, ruled the school with a rod of iron. He was over six feet tall with a large dome head accentuated by his receding hairline. Nobody talked in his presence so when he swept down the school corridor, with his black gown flailing behind him, the noise and bustle would progressively fade like the volume control on a radio being turned down. He had taught Liam English in his last two years and whilst he had always been grudging and sparing in his praise, Liam was not surprised at his forceful reaction on hearing that he was leaving at the end of term. The head was known for railing against this squandering of talent that happened annually.

'I'm sorry but I can't.' Liam felt his cheeks burning and he stood miserably looking down at the threadbare carpet. He felt the headmaster's eyes on him and there was a long silence in his study.

'All right but if your circumstances should change come and discuss things with me.' There was a resignation and tiredness in the headmaster's voice. He knew about Liam's present circumstances and how pointless it would be to discuss the matter further.

But ambition burned within Liam. He may have given the impression in the headmaster's study of downtrodden acquiescence, but for all his youthfulness Liam knew what was at stake. His mother, in the last year of her life had impressed upon him, with a burning intensity, that education was his ticket out of his present environment and Liam was determined to pursue it. He just didn't know how.

After the plain fare of fried fish and potatoes was eaten, Liam cleared the table and set about washing the dishes. The meal had been eaten in silence except for the noisy chewing of his stepfather which sounded like someone treading through a marshy field in wellington boots.

As he stood by the sink Liam warily watched his stepfather. The period after the evening meal was a difficult time and Liam hated it. During the day it was easy to stay out of his orbit. But in the evening, they were confined to the single living area of the house with the kitchen in one part and the lounge area in the rest of the room. Two heavy, brown settees, positioned on either side of the open fireplace dominated the small living space. Now that his mother was gone these evenings had become intolerable with Liam constantly on edge, fearing his stepfather's volatile temper and vicious tongue.

But this was Friday evening, traditionally the night that Meade went to the pub in the village on the other side of the estuary. These evenings were a mixed blessing. While it provided relief from the long-drawn-out, strained atmosphere that was now the norm, Meade would often come home drunk in an angry and twisted mood, and on these occasions his frustration and bitterness would erupt upon Liam.

'Get the boat ready?' Meade's snappy demand settled the

uncertainty. It was Liam's job to ensure that the small rowing boat was kept in a state of constant readiness. This was not onerous as it simply meant that the boat was pulled up onto the shore, made secure to a metal ring driven into the ground and covered in a tarpaulin to keep out the rain.

Liam didn't reply but he started to pull on his boots. Meade crossed the room and flung open the front door, letting in a blast of cold air; the sharp tangy air was impregnated by the smell of rotting fish carried downwind from the harbour and overhead was the constant squawking of the gulls. He stepped outside and looked around.

'I don't know. The sky's heavy. I think there's a storm brewing,' he muttered almost to himself as he stepped back over the threshold.

Liam said nothing but busied himself in the kitchen. Meade stood pondering for a few minutes and then abruptly turned to Liam: 'Right. Let's go now. It's starting to blow so I want ye to come for me early tonight. Nine o'clock sharp. Have ye got that?'

Liam nodded, careful not to show his pleasure that the matter was finally settled.

It required both of them to push the boat down the beach to the shore. It had not been used for a while and had settled into the wet sand but it gave Meade the opportunity to berate Liam for his lack of physical strength.

'You couldn't push your granny downstairs,' taunted Meade. 'The only job you'll get is cleaning the fish, along with the auld women.'

Liam said nothing but looked steadily at Meade. The unspoken challenge in that gaze was clear. *Time is not on your side, old man. I'm getting bigger and stronger every day and one day I'm going to stuff your insults down your throat until your face turns purple and your eyes are popping out of your head!*

But today was not the day, and Liam soon lowered his gaze and obediently and silently busied himself with the oars and rearranging the rigging.

The estuary was perhaps no more than 300 yards wide and on a normal day it would take no more than 10 minutes to row the boat directly across to the tiny inn, whose welcoming lights were clearly visible. To go by road required walking back through the village, over a small wooden bridge and then up the narrow road on the other side. A journey that would take almost an hour of brisk walking, a form of exercise that Meade avoided if he could.

Liam pulled at the oars while Meade lounged in the stern. He carefully pulled out his tobacco pouch and proceeded to sprinkle a thin layer along the thin cigarette paper.

'The good news is that I've got ye a job.' Meade paused deliberately, relishing the impact of his words. He licked the white cigarette paper along its length, rolled it closed and studied it briefly before slipping it into his mouth.

'The bad news is it's with auld McCauley.' Meade sniggered briefly before glancing up at Liam. 'He's the only one taking on deckhands. And since you've got f**k all experience, ye're lucky to get it.' Meade's tone turned harsh and try as he could Liam couldn't hide the stricken expression on his face. 'Be at his boat at 5 a.m. tomorrow.' And with that, Meade turned to the side and drew heavily on his thin cigarette. Conversation was at an end.

For Liam the news was devastating. He always dreaded the idea of a life on the boats, the danger, the cold and the squalid nature of trawling the nets and bringing up teems of gleaming, slippery fish, which have to be roughly gutted while they lay flapping on a large steel table. He remembered from his one isolated trip last summer the overpowering smell of diesel and fish, the constant lurching of the vessel and the thin layer of slime and grease that covered everything.

It was a perfect environment for blunting and corrupting human sensibilities. Liam's friend Rob, who was a year older than Liam, but a fellow soulmate at school with whom Liam shared books and discussions of the latest films, had joined his uncle's fishing fleet a year ago. When Liam met him recently, he was immediately struck by the void that had opened between them; Rob was loud, crude and boastful of his drinking exploits and his success with girls. To Liam, everything about him had coarsened and there were no longer any points of mutual interest.

Liam guided the boat to a set of steps beside the small quay and held on to a metal ring while Meade scrambled up the steps.

'Nine o'clock sharp,' he grunted and made his way quickly to the lights of the tavern where loud conversation and the sound of a fiddle tuning up could be heard.

Alone at last with his thoughts Liam slumped back on his

boat, overwhelmed by misery and loneliness; he felt tears welling up as he remembered his mother. She would not have allowed this to happen. While Meade's bullying had increased as his mother's health had deteriorated, she was still able to assert herself when the occasion demanded it.

Liam was jolted out of his reverie by the rocking of his boat and the slapping sound of the water against the side. The dusk had settled in and the wind was causing all the other boats in the harbour to start gently bobbing. When he looked through the ragged concrete entrance of the harbour and across the estuary, he could see the twinkling lights of the few cottages on the hillside and the white surf crashing against the shoreline. At this time of the year the estuary would normally be as still as blackened glass but now the wind was rippling the surface, creating flashes of white spume.

Liam decided that it was too risky to row back home and then return again for nine. Better to stay here and let Meade decide whether it was safe to make the crossing. If truth be told Liam was more frightened of Meade's temper, should he fail to be there at nine, rather than the danger that the double crossing on his own may pose.

But over and above all these considerations was the thought that he may be able to meet up with Rosaline. She was in his year at school and the gentle academic rivalry, with both of them competing for the top grades, had actually brought them together and emphasised their common interests, especially in literature. She was not pretty in the conventional sense, her face too angular and her nose a little too long, but she had long auburn hair, which in bright sunlight reflected a ginger tint like a seam of gold buried in dark soil, and her green eyes sparkled with humour and challenge. In his last term of school, they had become an 'item' and Liam had walked her home whenever his domestic circumstances allowed it.

Liam quickly tied the boat to the metal ring and mounted the concrete step to the quayside. Turning the opposite direction from the tavern, he walked along cobbled streets until he met the main road with its single streetlamp casting a hazy orange glow across the junction. As he turned left and walked along the side of the road, he could just make out the darkened silhouettes of the large houses set back from the road with their square solid frontage. Rosaline's house was second from the end standing four square in an elevated position above the road. He could see that the lights were on in the main lounge through the gaps in the curtains; there was also a light above the entrance of the door.

Liam stopped at the entrance of the driveway. His heart was beating nervously and his mouth was dry. How could he suddenly appear at their door at this time of the evening? What reason could he give? When he had walked Rosaline home, they would spend time sitting on the harbour wall talking and although Rosaline had invited him into her house Liam had always been under too much pressure to get home.

The door was a solid wood construction befitting of such a grand house and at eye level there was a large brass knocker. Liam hesitated before giving it a timid rap. He stood momentarily debating whether to knock again and louder or simply to abandon the exercise when suddenly light poured through the fanlight above the door. Rosaline's father appeared silhouetted against the hall light.

'Yes?' he said in a tone that was not unfriendly.

'I am sorry for disturbing you, sir, but I am a friend of Rosaline and I wonder if I could speak to her.' Liam was all too conscious of the nervousness in his voice.

There was a pause and Liam felt that he was being assessed.

'Hold on. Rosaline,' he shouted and then louder, 'Rosaline. There is someone here for you.'

A door opened and Rosaline appeared looking a little bewildered.

'Hi,' said Liam awkwardly, now feeling embarrassed at his impulsive action of turning up unexpectedly and in the dark as well.

'Oh, hi,' said Rosaline, a faint colour rising in her cheeks. Mercifully her father turned and left them to it.

'Sorry for turning up like this, but I had to drop my stepfather off at the tavern and I thought I would…' Liam's voice tailed off.

'That's all right. Why don't you come in?' Rosaline smiled and she at least seemed to have regained her composure.

Liam followed her down the corridor and into a room dominated by a large piano at one end and a settee and several chairs at the other end. A coal fire crackled in between.

'My mother gives piano lessons and this is the room she

uses. But all lessons are over for tonight, thank God.' Rosaline laughed. 'Would you like some tea?'

'Thank you but I'm OK,' Liam said, looking appreciatively round the room. Everything oozed middle-class comfort and solidity and Liam marvelled that they could set aside a room just for music lessons.

'Has your stepfather changed his mind about not allowing you to continue at school?' asked Rosaline, looking earnestly at Liam. Suddenly the pent-up emotions and frustrations of the past few days welled up and to his embarrassment he felt his eyes filling with tears. He looked away quickly and tried to control the tremble in his voice.

'No, things are even worse,' and then Liam proceeded to tell her of the deckhand job that Meade had secured and of how Meade was determined that he take it and start earning his keep. Under Rosaline's sympathetic gaze and gentle prodding Liam described how horrendous the last few months had been ever since his mother died. When he finished, he felt a sense of relief that he was able to unburden himself to someone. He glanced up at Rosaline and saw her staring at him with an unfocused gaze. 'Sit here,' she commanded. 'I'm going to speak to my father.'

Left to himself, Liam got up and wandered over to the bookshelf. It was full of musical scores and books on music and musicians. The sturdy upright piano had a well-used look about it with music sheets and magazines scattered on top along with the hint of a coffee mug stain at the far end. The walls had a medley of family photos and pictures of the village and the estuary from at least 50 years ago. He could hear the distant chimes of a grandfather clock at the far end of the house.

Liam was examining a family photo, trying to pick out a much younger image of Rosaline when he heard the door behind him opening.

'Well, young man, I believe that you may be looking for part-time work.' Rosaline's father strode into the room followed by Rosaline. Like all self-made small businessmen, he carried himself with an air of self-importance which bordered on the pompous. He was small, stocky with black hair cut unfashionably short and a nose much too large for its face. His saving grace was a pair of bright blue eyes, which were now appraising Liam, but were friendly, and even had the hint of an amused twinkle in them.

'Yes, sir. I'd like to stay on at school but I need to bring in some money into the family home.' Liam was taken aback by the directness of the father's question as he had never discussed this possibility with Rosaline but, with his pulse quickening, he quickly realised the possibility on offer.

'And very commendable too,' the father said, reflectively stroking his long nose. 'What hours do you think you can manage?'

Liam thought quickly. No point in working part-time if he was unable to keep up with his school work. And then Meade would want him to do his more than fair share of the housework.

'Three hours after school and all day Saturday,' but even as he said it, Liam realised with a sinking heart that Meade would never agree to it. It represented less than half the hours he would work on the trawler and that was not counting the bonus trawler men could earn based on the size of a catch; and then there was the long-standing tradition that allowed them to take some fish home for personal consumption. Meade had got progressively lazier ever since Liam's mother died; he would spend days on end lying on the couch, smoking and reading the horse racing pages and would only reluctantly stir himself to go looking for some part-time work when fags, beer or basic provisions had run out. Liam knew with absolute certainty that Meade had always wanted Liam to start work as soon as he could be withdrawn legally from school and that he would never countenance any diminution in Liam's earning potential.

Liam face must have reflected the turmoil that he was feeling.

'What's the matter?' said Rosaline gently; her steady gaze was warm and sympathetic.

'He'll not agree to it,' said Liam bitterly. 'He wants me working full-time so he can retire and spend his time in the pub.' Once again Liam felt his tears starting to sting his eyes and he looked away, embarrassed. There was a long moment of silence interrupted by the ticking of a large clock on the mantlepiece.

'Well let's not give up at the first hurdle,' said Rosaline's father briskly. 'Would it help if I spoke to him?' he asked.

'No,' replied Liam quickly. He was only too aware of his

stepfather's contrary nature; he would certainly resent any interference into what he would regard as a private matter, no matter how well meaning. And anyway, what could be said that would convince him to give up his meal ticket! Once again, they all fell silent and Liam was aware of Rosaline's gaze as it switched anxiously from looking at both of them.

'Look, we're not going to sort anything out tonight. Let me think about this. I may need to speak to your headmaster, is that all right?'

Liam thought quickly. 'OK, but please don't say anything to my stepfather… at least not yet.'

Liam walked quickly back, retracing his steps to the tavern. His mind was in a whirl thinking of the discussion and the possibilities; despite the known difficulties he could not suppress a feeling of hope. His predicament and the selfish attitude of Meade was now out there; Rosaline's father was a magistrate and a councillor and well known in the community. Liam thought if anyone could do something, then he could.

There was a loud murmur of conversation punctured with laughter as Liam approached the tavern. The heavy main door was slightly ajar and that led into a small vestibule where on the left was a door with the word *Lounge* inscribed along the top and straight ahead an identical door with the word *Bar* on the top. Pausing for a moment to gather his composure, Liam pushed opened the door marked *Bar* and was momentarily taken aback by the dense, smoky atmosphere caused by the open fireplace and old Barney

Crothers puffing away at his stumpy pipe. The bar, brightly lit, was at the far end of the room, running along most of the length, with a parallel overhanging shelf on which beer glasses were neatly arranged.

The room was crowded with men standing and sitting in small groups; most of them were sea men or harbour workers and all of them with the week's pay in their pockets. It was a jolly atmosphere but Liam was in no mood to enjoy it as he looked around the room. Meade was easy to spot standing at the left-hand end of the bar. Suddenly, Liam realised, with a sickening lurch to his heart, that Meade was with auld McCauley. They were standing close together with Meade's hand on McCauley's shoulder and talking animatedly into his right ear. Liam instinctively drew back but it was too late as McCauley saw him and turned in his direction, prompting Meade to look over as well.

'My new shipmate! Come over here and let's have a better luk at ye,' McCauley shouted over, causing a few bystanders to look round. Liam sidled over and McCauley put an arm round his shoulders and pulled him closer in a show of faux bonhomie. 'We'll soon put a bit of muscle on these,' he said, giving Liam's arms a squeeze. There was something utterly repellent about McCauley; he had a heavy grey stubble, small piglike blue eyes whose coldness and watchfulness belied the big welcoming smile; but it was his thick lips and the way the bottom lip hung down, moist and slack almost with a sexual lasciviousness. Liam edged away but McCauley kept a possessive arm on his shoulder.

'All set for tomorrow morning?'

Liam nodded in what he hoped was an uncommitted way but misery was written across his face. Meade noticed it and could not help snapping, 'And be there bright and early with a smile on yer gob. You're lucky to get a job. You've no experience and you're soft.'

'Ach, now don't be hard on the boy, we all have to start at the bottom.' McCauley's breath reeked of stout and tobacco and his physical nearness ensured the full blast of his body odour. Liam instinctively stepped away and McCauley let his arm slip off his shoulders in almost a caress.

'I think we better go. It's quite blowy outside,' Liam said.

'It's quite blowy, is it?' mimicked Meade. 'Well, you haven't seen anything yet. Wait until ye are out of the harbour and the other side of the Skerries, then you'll know what blowing is. Isn't that right, Patrick?'

'Now don't be scaring the lad, Donal,' McCauley replied, his mean little eyes appraising and predatory. 'We'll make a great sailor of him in no time.'

It was more than just blowing when they eventually got out of the pub. A frustrating process as Meade stopped to chat with various men as they weaved their way between the tables. Outside Liam could see that even Meade was taken aback by the gusts but he stubbornly ploughed on to the quayside. Earlier, the boats in the harbour had been gently bobbing, but now they were thrashing backwards and forward, straining at their moors like wild animals fighting to be free of their leash. Meade stood contemplating his small boat which was bucking up and down by the harbour wall. It was dark, but a bright full moon lit up the lagoon beyond and it was not difficult to make out the foam-crested swell. To Liam it was clearly too dangerous to attempt the crossing but he stood there keeping his counsel, only too aware of Meade's perverse and capricious nature.

Meade hesitated and he was clearly concerned about the swell.

'Now Donal, you can't pass up this opportunity to show young Liam a bit of action, now, can ye?' McCauley's wheedling voice came out of the darkness. 'It'll help to toughen him up by tomorrow, so I don't have a whimpering wee girl on board.' McCauley's tone suddenly took on a harsh ring as he stepped into the overhead street light, slightly swaying on his feet, with a half-filled glass of stout in his hand. 'Get in the boat,' snapped Meade to Liam. He was clearly annoyed that McCauley had put him in a position where his own courage and seamanship was being challenged but under the guise of creating a test for Liam. Large spots of rain started to fall, adding to the wildness of the scene, but rather than causing any rethink it only added to Meade's sense of urgency. 'Get into the f*****g boat,' he shouted. But now Liam was very fearful; he could see that the swell beyond the harbour entrance and he knew that his stepfather was in no fit state to take the boat out in these conditions.

'No. It's far too rough. Let's walk and I'll pick up the boat tomorrow.' Liam had never disobeyed a direct command from Meade before, but if he'd to make a start then this was certainly a good time.

'Well, well! It looks as if you've a mutiny on your hands here, Donal. You know that can't be tolerated.' McCauley's tone was mocking, he was clearly enjoying Meade's discomfort. 'In my boat that would get you the birch.'

'Come here, you gutless little mammy's boy.' Meade stood up on the boat and made a grab for Liam's arm to drag him into the boat. But Liam pulled back and Meade swayed dangerously as the boat violently rocked beneath him. For a moment it looked like he'd recovered his equilibrium when suddenly he started swinging his arms frantically before toppling back, hitting the side of the boat and rolling into the water.

For a moment Liam and McCauley stood frozen in horror as Meade's head surfaced and he started threshing the water. Like all local sailors he kept faith with the age-old seafaring superstition and had never learnt to swim.

'Get in the boat quick and we'll get him,' cried McCauley, who with commendable speed had started down the harbour steps.

McCauley cast off and Liam grabbed the oars to steer the boat towards Meade who was now twenty yards away, being sucked by the tide towards the harbour entrance. He was still thrashing the water but his cries for help were now more of a loud gurgling as he struggled for air. Liam was initially terrified by the events that were unfolding and reacted swiftly, when a thought entered his head and would not go away. *If Meade died all his problems disappeared. No deckhand skivvy with*

McCauley. No leaving school early.

'For f***'s sake, row harder,' snarled McCauley, 'and more to the left.' Liam instinctively obeyed and then regretted it as the boat drew alongside the struggling figure who was now regularly disappearing under the water. McCauley reached down and grabbed Meade by the scruff of his jacket and pulled so that his head was above water. The boat tipped precariously on one side as McCauley leaned over and fought to keep a semi-conscious Meade afloat.

'Now row back to the steps,' gasped McCauley. He was on one knee and balanced precariously hanging over the side, his face showing the physical strain of holding on to a figure, which still struggled for its life. Liam thought quickly as he leaned forward slowly to pick up the oar, which was lying on the bottom of the boat close to McCauley. He had to half rise out of his seat to get it, which caused the boat to tip further on its side. In a flash Liam threw himself against the bent back of McCauley. McCauley let go of Meade and as he toppled over the side, he twisted round to grab the side of the boat, which was now rocking furiously. He managed to get his left hand onto the side of the boat and was struggling to twist round and free his right hand. But Meade was hanging onto McCauley with all the desperation of a drowning man. McCauley's cries for help were now added to Meade's gurgling sounds. Surely someone would hear them on the shore.

McCauley let go of the boat in a desperate attempt to free himself from Meade's deathly grasp and Liam took the opportunity to gently paddle the boat away from the drowning figures. His last image was of McCauley's upturned face with eyes, wide open in terror, which seemed to look directly at Liam in a silent cry for help.

Liam sat in the boat his heart pounding as he watched the two figures locked in a deadly embrace with only their heads showing above the moonlit water. The wind and the swell within the harbour had, if anything, increased and Liam watched in frozen fascination as their heads would briefly appear and then disappear in the swell. They did not appear to be making any sounds anymore, or maybe it was drowned out by the wind. Then abruptly he could no longer see them. Liam intently scanned where they were last seen, afraid to blink least he might miss them. How long he sat there, almost in a trance, he could not say but eventually he started back to the harbour steps where it all started. He needed to collect his thoughts. He needed to get his story together.

*

Sir Robert L. Maitland leaned forward in the back seat of his Daimler saloon. This was not easy as the back seats were angled to encourage the passenger to slide back into their comfortable embrace. He leaned forward on their edge as the car nosed its way down the high street and scanned from side to side for any familiar landmark or building, but so much had changed.

'Stop here,' he snapped to his chauffeur, a young man whose thick, long, black hair made his chauffeur cap perch ludicrously on top of his head in a manner which invited ridicule. How he missed old Thomas who had been with him for over twenty years and shared the same generational values and attitude. But he wanted to retire and this young guy – *What's his name? Oh, Jason* – was the best of a bad bunch.

'I'll walk. Park somewhere here where I can find you. I'll be about half an hour.'

'OK, boss.' Sir Robert grimaced at the casual response which to his ears sounded less than respectful; old Thomas always called him by his title. Sir Robert. A resounding title and certainly made him glad that he had switched his middle name to his forename. Sir Liam didn't quite cut it.

The air had a chilly autumnal sharpness and Sir Robert pulled the collar of his long black overcoat up to his ears. He looked around for someone to ask, but the road was deserted except for an elderly couple who were some yards away and walking in the opposite direction. Crossing the road, he spotted a signpost and when he got closer it had an arrow indicating the direction of the harbour.

'Just what I'm looking for,' he murmured and turned down the side road. This road soon narrowed to barely the width of a car and, with no pavement, Sir Robert walked carefully down it, checking frequently over his shoulder that no traffic was coming.

The sudden brightness of the broad expanse of the harbour promenade, after the narrow road, brought him up short; this was not as he'd remembered it. But gradually he realised that all the old warehouses, which had previously cluttered the promenade with their equipment and fishing nets and low-level wooden sheds, had disappeared along with the demise of the small fishing fleet. Sir Robert scanned the promenade from one end to the other trying to get his bearing; there were coffee bars, bistros and expensive fish restaurants but nothing that resembled the tavern of his youth.

He decided to walk to the end of the promenade closest to the entrance of the harbour, the place where he believed he had disembarked that fateful night. This part of the promenade retained the old cobblestones and the concrete bollards for securing the ships. As he approached the end of the promenade, he felt the wind strongly on his face and he could see beyond the entrance of the harbour to the open estuary and across the estuary to the line of houses where he'd once lived.

He looked over the edge of the harbour and allowed his eye to scan along the wall. And then he spotted it, less than 10 yards from where he stood. The narrow steps, set into the wall of the harbour, giving access to the water edge. They had a forlorn, forgotten air about them, the hand rail deeply rusted and the last two steps covered in a slippery, green moss. Fifty years ago he had raced up these steps.

*

For weeks he had dreaded the inquest, convinced that something would emerge during the hearing that would undermine his carefully rehearsed account of the evening in question. When he raised the alarm by dashing into the tavern that night, everyone was of a one in their sympathy and support; even the policemen, who interviewed him a few days later, simply recorded the events as he reported them and did not dig any deeper.

'You've nothing to blame yourself about, son,' said Sergeant McGrath, as he snapped closed his little black notebook. 'Two big grown-up men like that, struggling for their life in the water… even a big strong man probably couldn't have saved them.'

Meade's body was found several days later washed down towards the mouth of the estuary; McCauley's body was never recovered and the general view was that it had been carried out into the Irish Sea. The coroner, Mr. Hawkins, was a large man with bushy eyebrows, and a long mournful face who always wore a dark suit and waistcoat with a gold watch chain. He relished his position and, as this case had attracted widespread interest in the community, he conducted himself with more than his usual solemn authority. In a slow and deliberate voice, he explained that the purpose of this court was to establish the cause of death by hearing of the circumstances that surrounded the death; he would not be trying to ascertain if anyone was responsible for the death as this was not a trial. The likely outcome would be one of the following: accident, suicide, unlawful killing, or open verdict. As there was only one witness to the events, he would be called shortly to give his evidence.

Liam's mouth suddenly went dry at the prospect and he felt that he might be sick. He was very conscious of all the people in the public gallery who would be listening carefully to every word that he said, including Rosaline, her father and his old headmaster Mr. Weatherall. Liam knew that there was a big silver lining in this cloud for him, but one verbal slip in recounting his evidence and a deep shadow of doubt would be cast over his role. The events of the past week, the police investigation, the lead-up to the inquest, the funeral arrangements for Meade, had allowed Liam not to think of that fateful night or to dwell on the plain fact that he had murdered McCauley. It was not premediated; it was a spontaneous act but nevertheless he had killed a man.

He had a few moments to regain his composure while a statement from the landlord of the tavern was read out. He simply confirmed that both men had been drinking steadily in the pub for most of the evening and whilst they were not 'falling down drunk' they had consumed a fair amount of alcohol. And then it was Liam's turn.

As he stood up on the witness stand, he felt that all eyes were on him and there was a rustle of expectancy as people leaned forward to hear what he had to say.

'Can you please confirm your name?' asked the coroner. Liam did so, conscious of the tremble in his voice. 'Thank you. Now we appreciate that this must be a very difficult time for you but it's important that this court understands fully the events of the evening in question. Can you please tell the court what happened in your own words and take your time.'

Liam's voice grew stronger as he once again took up the story commencing with leaving the pub with Meade. He'd told the story many times, so that he was now word perfect. And he was determined to stick to the script. At the crucial point, when he described how Meade in his desperation had pulled McCauley over the side, he glanced up at the coroner and noticed that he was watching Liam intently. There was something a little disconcerting in that concentrated gaze which set off an alarm bell. In all previous occasions, when he had to relate the events of that night, he was greeted with encouragement and support with no intrusive questions asked. Now he felt it might be different and it was with a feeling of apprehension that he ended his account.

'Thank you, Mr. Maitland,' the coroner said. 'It's important for this court to understand the state of mind and the relationships between the people involved in this tragic affair. I realise that some of my questions may require you to express an opinion and therefore your answer will be a subjective one. The court will understand this, but…' Hawkins paused and looked over to where the public was sitting. He was clearly enjoying himself. 'Nevertheless, we need to go beyond the simple facts of this case, to assure ourselves of the conclusion that we are going to make. However, I need to emphasise that no one is on trial here. We simply wish to get a rounded picture of all the circumstances.'

Hawkins paused and rearranged some of the papers on his desk.

'I understand that you live with Mr. Meade and that his wife, your mother, died nine months ago.'

'That is correct,' replied Liam.

'And how would you describe the state of Mr. Meade after your mother died?'

'How do you mean?' stammered Liam.

'Did he seem depressed, anxious, preoccupied…'

'Sad, I guess,' said Liam, but he knew that Meade was actually relieved and said as much. He was no longer subject to his mother's disdainful gaze or her sharp tongue.

'And how long did his period of bereavement last?'

'Not long,' Liam said shortly. There was no mistaking the sharpness of Liam's tone and the coroner had not missed it.

'And how well did you get on with your stepfather?' he asked.

Liam paused and then said, 'We co-existed.' Liam could not bring himself to be any more diplomatic than that. He felt disturbed by this line of questioning and was unsure on how best to respond. But everyone in that courtroom was in no doubt that they did not get on.

'How often did you transport your stepfather across the estuary?'

'Every week depending on the weather,' Liam replied.

'Now what do you know about the relationship between your stepfather and Mr. McCauley?'

'I don't know much but I believe they were friends,' replied Liam.

'I understand that your stepfather asked Mr. McCauley for a job for you on his fishing boat?' Liam was stunned by the question. He cursed the small town's gossipy culture where nothing could be kept secret. He hesitated before replying.

'I believe so… I don't know for sure,' but even as he said it, he was conscious of how disingenuous he sounded.

'And how did you feel about the job offer?' Hawkins was relentless.

'I don't know. I hadn't thought too much about it.' By this time Liam's face was burning and he felt a trickle of sweat down the side of his face. What a stupid answer to give! Rosaline and her father were perfectly aware that he had been with them that fateful night, railing against the nightmare of working as a ship's cabin boy on McCauley's boat. They must wonder why he'd given such an evasive reply.

And then suddenly it was all over. The coroner thanked Liam for his contribution and Liam, momentarily confused by the sudden end of the proceedings, stumbled out of the witness box.

'There will be a short adjournment while I consider what I've heard,' Hawkins said ponderously.

There was a shuffling of feet and several members of the public left. Rosaline took the opportunity to slip in beside him.

'That must have been horrible for you. You did very well,' she said encouragingly in a whisper.

'I didn't know how best to answer the last questions,' Liam whispered back. 'I felt I was on trial.'

He looked carefully around the courtroom. It was full of members of the town, many of whom he knew, at least by sight. The tragedy of two local fishermen drowning within their own harbour had attracted widespread interest not only within the community but further afield. He noticed a newspaper reporter who had already tried to interview him about the accident. He'd declined, citing that he'd been advised not to speak to the press until after the coroner's verdict. Now, Liam felt that he would be gagging at the bit and bound to start poking at the new information revealed by the coroner's questions. He was certain that everyone would have picked up from the abruptness in his response that there was no love lost between him and Meade. Now add on the new dimension of the job offer and the prevaricating nature of his response and suspicions were surely bound to have been sowed. Liam looked nervously around and caught Rosaline's father looking at him. He was sure that he had a quizzical look on his face.

'All stand,' the usher shouted and everyone in the court room stood as the coroner returned to the room. Hawkins sat down, opened the folder in front of him, paused to look round the courtroom, clearly savouring his moment, and then commenced:

'I need hardly say that this was a dreadful event which resulted in the death of two men, hardworking fishermen, from our community. Our sincere condolences to the relatives and friends of both men.' Hawkins paused and looked over the top of his glasses before continuing. 'I've carefully reviewed the police report and the evidence of our only witness, Mr. Maitland, and have concluded that Mr. Meade and Mr. McCauley both died as the result of accidental drowning. The court would wish to acknowledge the personal bravery of Mr. McCauley who selflessly tried to rescue his friend and who perished as a result.' The coroner stopped and carefully took off his reading glasses before saying, 'And that concludes the verdict of this court.'

Outside the courthouse Liam stood in a small circle with Rosaline, her father, his old headmaster and a solicitor who Rosaline's father had encouraged and facilitated the appointment of to represent Liam's interest. A light drizzle was falling which only added to the greyness of the occasion.

'Well. No surprises there,' the young solicitor said, rubbing his hands. He had sandy-coloured hair that was thinning on top, pointy features and small protruding teeth, all of which conveyed the impression of a nervous rodent. 'We can now get a death certificate and start sorting out the estate.'

Liam could only nod numbly as his mind was in a whirl after the experience. He needed time on his own to sort out his thoughts and feelings. The coroner's unexpected line of questions, which had revealed the offer of a job with McCauley and Liam's patent lack of enthusiasm for it, had shaken him.

'Please tell me that he didn't suffer.' The plaintive voice came from behind and when Liam turned around, he saw a small, elderly woman whose narrow lined face was enclosed in a tightly worn head scarf. She was wearing a stained beige overcoat that was away too big for her and which reached down to the tips of her toes. However, it was her eyes, which held Liam's gaze, they were small and black and bore into him with a fierce intensity.

'I'm sorry…?' said Liam, momentarily confused.

'Mr. McCauley was my husband. I listened to you in the court but they never went into much detail about his last moments. Please, can you tell me again about it but more slowly. You see he was all I had and I just can't believe he's gone.' She cut such a forlorn figure with her oversized overcoat and head scarf that Liam felt a surge of sympathy for her. Behind her stood a young man, that Liam recognised as McCauley's son, Conor, a known troublemaker who had already done time for grievous bodily assault. It was well known that he and his father did not get on, but here he now was the dutiful son, his father's death having reawakened his filial loyalty. He stood behind his mother and regarded Liam with a hard stare.

'It all happened so quickly, I'm not sure if I can add much more,' said Liam.

'But how did he fall in? My Patrick was such a strong man. He could lift his fishing tackle with one hand. Nobody else could do that. His friends can't understand why he couldn't lift Mr. Meade into the boat.'

'I suppose he lost his balance. The boat was rocking about at the time.' Liam was conscious that the rest of the group was listening to what he said.

'My father was born in a rocking boat. He could stay on his feet in a force six,' snapped McCauley's son, Conor. 'And anyway, why couldn't he clamber back on board? He's fallen overboard enough in his time.'

'Maybe because my stepfather was clinging on to him,' Liam replied, conscious that both wife and son were watching his face intently.

'And what were you doing at the time?' The son's questions were starting to sound accusatory and Liam felt himself flushing again as he had done under questioning at the inquest.

'I tried to steer the boat to where they were drifting,' stammered Liam, feeling that his response sounded weak and inadequate. But he knew that it was better than the truth, that he had deliberately steered his boat away from the struggling figures!

'And did you get close to them?' The son was relentless.

'I think so. I couldn't see very well.' Liam knew as soon as the words had left his mouth that he had allowed the first crack to appear on his narrative.

'If my father had been able to get a hand onto the boat nothing would have prised him off. You panicked and you let them drown.' McCauley's son's voice had now a distinctly hard edge to it.

'Excuse me. I think we're all a little overwrought.' Rosaline's father stepped forward; they had all been listening with scarcely concealed rapt attention. 'It's been a terrible tragedy for your family and for Liam. No one is to blame. It has simply been a terrible accident.'

McCauley's son didn't reply but continued to stare hard at Liam.

'Please excuse my son. He means no offense,' his mother chimed in. She had an ingratiating tone, which was well practiced over the years but at odds with her tight mouth and hard eyes. 'But you see, we find it difficult to believe what happened. For us, there are many unanswered questions.' With this parting shot she beckoned her son and turned and walked away.

Her son, after a short hesitation followed her, but not before deliberately brushing past Liam and hissing in his face, 'Coward!'

Liam stood there motionless, close to tears. He was drained and shocked by all that had happened. Firstly, the coroner's probing and now this confrontation, which had portrayed him as a cowardly individual whose panic-stricken response to the plight of the men in the water led to them drowning. Surely someone would link these snippets of information together and conclude that there was more to this 'accident' than met the eye.

'Well, I think this is enough for one day.' Rosaline's father had stepped forward from the group to where Liam was standing. 'People often get very emotional at a coroner's proceedings. They say things that they don't mean. In a few days things will have calmed down.'

But they never did! Young McCauley set out to persecute him. There could be no other word to describe the orchestrated campaign of lies and outright physical intimidation that he suffered. Whenever he got the chance, he would physically confront Liam, pushing and shoving him, challenging him to respond, while all the time spitting in his face the word, *'Coward!'* Conor lost no time in constructing an account of the incident, which he repeated endlessly to any audience that he found. In Conor's version of events, Liam had cowardly failed to steer the boat towards the struggling men, fearful that if he gave any assistance the boat would be capsized. According to Conor, he'd watched the men drown rather than help them.

And Conor McCauley did not let it rest with just spreading lies and innuendo around the village, he also deliberately targeted Liam's school, often waiting outside the gates to shout abuse at him whenever school ended. If the pupils in the school had not already heard of the allegation, they were soon apprised of it. On one terrible occasion, Liam came home to his house only to find the word *gutless* scrawled in large yellow letters across the front wall of his house.

It is an axiom of any propaganda campaign that if you repeat a lie often enough, it will soon be uncritically accepted as the truth. And so Liam discovered as the weeks went past. He became ultra-sensitive to a certain coolness, a reserve, from his erstwhile school friends. On several occasions, he would come across them standing around chatting and then, on spotting his approach, they would fall self-consciously silent. Even Rosaline did not escape his inflamed sensitivity.

'You do believe me, don't you? That it was an accident that I couldn't prevent?' challenged Liam one day as they were walking home from school.

'Of course, I do. But in a small place like here these rumours are bound to do the rounds. Especially with Conor McCauley pumping out a new one every day.' It wasn't cowardice which dictated Liam's actions that night, but a ruthless and focused desire not to be sucked into the life of one-dimensional drudgery that his stepfather had mapped out.

Rosaline didn't know that Liam's solicitor had just informed him that probate had been settled and that he was now the owner of the property that he lived in, and that, once he was eighteen, he could dispose of it as he saw fit. For Liam, the exit route could not be clearer. He would finish his year at school and head for university or whatever, his independence secured by the proceeds of the sale of the house. He would cut all his ties with this place. Leave and never come back.

*

But here he was, back almost half a century later!! Sir Robert found it difficult to explain his motivation even to himself. Certainly, there were no old acquaintances that he wanted to look up. Rosaline and he had drifted apart after they both went to different universities in distant parts of the country. He had short-lived pangs of remorse at how he'd deliberately let the relationship slide, delaying answering her letters, steadfastly refusing any invitation to stay with her family over the term breaks and so on; eventually it was Rosaline who formally broke the relationship after a tearful phone call. He felt liberated afterwards, although he recognised that, in this instance, he was being a coward. Many years later he heard by chance that she had married a French biologist and moved to France.

Steel had entered his soul that night in the harbour, and had then been tested and tempered in the months that followed with the campaign of vilification from young McCauley. Looking back, he realised that the experience had hardened him, it had blunted any sense of guilt. He had murdered a man who had done him no harm but he deliberately closed and locked the door on any thoughts of remorse. It made him ruthless, where relationships were seen through a transactional prism, and two short-lived marriages were a testament to his emotionally cold and flawed personality. It also made Sir Robert one of the most successful and feared men in the City.

But what made him come back? Sir Robert pondered this question as he sat on a wooden bench and watched the dark green harbour water flow gently into the estuary. Occasionally the sunlight would flash back a kaleidoscope of colour as it glanced a streak of oil floating on the surface. A seagull landed close by and wandered warily around, all the time keeping him under close observation through a cold, unblinking yellow eye. Suddenly it rose in a flurry of flapping wings and a loud complaining squawk as another figure sat down on the far end of the bench from Sir Robert.

'Nasty creatures. They tear open the rubbish bags, spread the rubbish around the town and that attracts the rats.' The new companion wore a baseball cap pulled over a thin face with hollow cheeks and a grey stubble. 'I don't know why people feed them. It only makes them bolder.' Sir Robert quickly appraised his new companion. Probably in his fifties, he wore a black suede jacket that looked decidedly threadbare in parts, a black T-shirt and denim trousers. The classic outfit for a native of the harbour, thought Sir Robert, sardonically.

'At least when we had a fishing fleet that kept them occupied... and fed,' Sir Robert replied.

'That's true. But that's some years ago.' His new companion had now half turned and was returning the appraisal. 'That must be going back at least twenty-five years ago. Did you know the town then?'

'No. I am talking nearly fifty years ago. I used to come down here for the summer and live with an uncle and aunt,' Sir Robert lied easily. He reckoned that this fellow was perhaps ten years younger than him, maybe more, but he did not wish to get sucked into any awkward questions. 'Do you live in the town?' he asked, gently steering the conversation away from him.

'I was born here and worked here for most of my life but moved away, for work, about eight years ago. I'm back visiting my sister,' he replied.

'I was friends with a big lad from the village when I stayed with my uncle. His name, if I remember correctly, was Conor McCauley. Did you know him?'

Sir Robert, when he reflected later, realised that finding McCauley was almost certainly the subconscious reason why he had taken the spur-of-the-moment decision to make a detour to see his old hunting ground. Now that he'd spoken his name out loud, he felt the old feelings of anger and resentment come surging back. For many years, the humiliations that McCauley had heaped upon him, he would use to fuel his relentless drive for success and made him view all competitors as McCauley-like figures for whom no quarter could be given until they were eliminated.

The man paused before replying. 'The only McCauleys I know own a small food production plant just outside the town, on the A470 on the left, after the first roundabout. I don't know them. I just see the big sign McCauley & Son on their side wall every time I'm driving home.'

'The McCauley I knew owned a small fishing boat. They may have changed their employment or they may be related. But thank you. I may follow it up.'

Sir Robert was lost in thought as he sat in the car staring unseeingly at the back of his chauffeur's head with his hair spilling out underneath his cap. The car's engine was running quietly as Jason waited for instruction. A quick call back to his office had established that the owner and managing director of this small food factory was no less a person than Conor McCauley. Here was the chance to confront the demon figure of his youth. Many times he had visualised this moment. No longer the fearful youth cowering under McCauley's bullying behaviour. No, by God, this would be Sir Robert, knight of the realm, rich and powerful who would look McCauley straight in the eye and tell him that he had deliberately pushed his odious father into the harbour and yes, he had rowed away so that he couldn't clamber back on board. And Sir Robert would then stare the fat bastard down, daring him to do something about it. *Let's see who has guts now!*

'Can you say it's a personal matter?' Sir Robert handed his card through the window of the small reception area and watched, in some amusement, as the young girl stared in some confusion at the card, embossed with his coat of arms and containing his full title and letters.

'I'll just be a moment,' she said, her cheeks starting to flush as she darted out of the door holding the card.

Sir Robert took in the whole reception area with a practiced eye; a small enterprise, probably employing no more than thirty staff, moderately successful but coasting along. No sense of energy or dynamism.

'Can you please come with me?' the receptionist said and immediately led Sir Robert along the corridor and up a flight of stairs. Despite his self-confidence, indeed arrogance, in the car, Sir Robert felt his pulse start to quicken and a small knot forming in his stomach. Would McCauley recognise the name on the card? How should he introduce himself? How would he start the conversation and lead it to his moment of denouement?

The young receptionist held open the door and Sir Robert strode in, bracing himself for this long-awaited confrontation. A middle-aged man stood up behind a small desk strewn with papers and files.

'Good afternoon, Sir Robert. What can I do for you?'

Sir Robert was momentarily speechless. Clearly this was not the McCauley of his youth.

'I think I may have to apologise. I used to live in this town in my youth and I've never been back. But a good friend in those days was a lad called Conor McCauley and when I saw the name on the wall of your factory, I thought I would call in the off chance…' Sir Robert ended, slightly embarrassed that his behaviour would appear unprofessional at the very least.

'No problem, No problem. I think you probably knew my father. He founded this business and lived here all his life. Unfortunately, he passed away just under a year ago. My name is also Conor McCauley, but I'm known in the family as Dominic. I'm his only son and I now run the business.'

'I'm sorry. I should've phoned,' Sir Robert replied, feeling a sense of disappointment and frustration starting to well up.

'As I said, it's not a problem. Can I offer you a drink, coffee or something stronger?'

'Thank you. But before I waste any more of your time, I should make certain that your father was my friend. The Conor I knew, his father died in a drowning accident in the harbour.'

'Yep, that's my father,' Dominic said. 'When did you know him? I don't recall him ever mentioning your name.'

'I was only here during the school holidays so I probably didn't make that much impression on him. Indeed, I think that the time of the accident was my last time here. That was a dreadful incident and I often wondered how your father and your grandmother coped,' Sir Robert said, angling to steer the conversation towards the topic of his obsession.

'If you were speaking to my father, he'd tell you that it was the making of him. You may know that he didn't get on with his father and neither did his mother. He seems to have been a bit of a brute by all accounts. Did you know that they never found his body?'

'Yes. I do remember that,' said Sir Robert, delighted that they had so quickly zoomed on to the topic of interest.

'Well,' continued Dominic, warming to his theme and delighted that such a distinguished figure was evidently interested in his story. Perhaps there could be a useful business connection here… 'Apparently old Grandad McCauley had taken out a life insurance policy only a year earlier, for a tidy sum too, and when no body was found the local tongues started to wag. The view was that he faked his drowning and that he was in hiding!'

'I've to say I never heard that rumour when I was here,' Sir Robert said, genuinely surprised. 'But wasn't there a witness to the drowning. A young lad from the town, whose stepfather was the other victim.'

'He was judged to be in it as well. It came out at the inquest that he was about to start work for my grandfather and that he hated his stepfather.' Dominic leaned back in his chair and beamed; he was clearly enjoying himself. 'You can see how a neat story of planning and collusion could be created.'

'That's astonishing. As I said, we never heard a whisper of that rumour,' Sir Robert said, his mind in a whirl.

'If you knew this fishing community that wouldn't surprise you. There's a long tradition of keeping our dirty linen out of view and sorting out our own problems, without involving the authorities, if you know what I mean,' Dominic said. 'Anyway, my father and my grandmother stuck it out, conscientiously acting the grieving family and eventually the insurance people paid up. That, along with the sale of the boat, allowed my father to set up this business.' Dominic concluded with a wave of his hand, intended to convey the vastness of the enterprise.

'I'm dumfounded,' said Sir Robert and meant it.

Later in the car Sir Robert tried to disentangle his thoughts and feelings. It seemed clear to him that McCauley's campaign of bullying was aimed at dispelling any rumour that there was any collusion between his family and him. It was not personal but calculating, something that Sir Robert could relate to. In fact, thinking about it objectively, the death of both men had cleared the way for all of them to prosper. It was like cutting out a cancer before it was able to destroy the life chances of the patient. It was a win-win result. Sir Robert started to feel a sense of absolution, as if he had been to confession and the priest had found a way for him to atone for a long-standing guilty action.

'Where to now, boss?' Jason asked.

'Let me show you, young man, where I was born.'

Jason looked up, startled at the unmistakable good humour in his boss's voice.

THE BROKEN WINDOW

My parents were delighted when I passed the eleven plus, known locally as the 'qually', a laconic abbreviation of its more formal title of 'The Qualify Examination of the Northern Ireland Educational Board.' I remember watching anxiously for the post and then pouncing on the envelope as it came through the letterbox. The rumour was that if you had failed, the envelope would be small and thin as it would simply contain a terse statement that you had not been successful. I cannot recall whether I took in the size or dimension of the brown envelope, only that my hands shook when I tore it open to read those memorable words 'We are delighted to inform you…'

My grammar school was situated in one of the worst areas of Belfast. It was at the other side of the city from where I lived, which meant a two-bus journey every day on a trolley bus, a form of transport almost unique to Belfast, which boasted the largest fleet of trolley buses in Europe. These vehicles would be popular with present-day environmentalists as they were powered by overhanging electrical cables. Every so often the bus rollers would get detached from the hanging cables, bringing the bus to an abrupt stop. The conductor would then have to retrieve a long pole, which had been stored the length of the bus, and hook the rollers back onto the cables. This would be no mean feat as the pole was long and heavy and he would be watched by an increasing number of passers-by, who would give a sardonic cheer every time he failed to connect to the cable.

The main road up to the school, from which the school got its name, was a rough, tough neighbourhood where the local kids would lie in wait for school end in order to give vent to their anger at this foreign entity in their midst. The school never participated in the local community but held itself apart, divided not only by the selection process but also by religion. For this was a Protestant grammar school in the middle of a staunchly republican part of Belfast.

Life for first-year pupils was decidedly miserable. Everything was new and strange and very intimidating. All the teachers wore black gowns and addressed pupils abruptly by their surname. We lived in terror of being subjected to the school's traditional initiation ritual. This consisted of being dragged off to the boys' toilets – aptly named the 'bogs' – by the older pupils and having your head forced down into the toilet bowl, which was then flushed to the gleeful delight of the participants.

In the midst of all this misery I struck up a friendship with a wiry, dark-haired boy called George who lived on the bus route so that we were able to meet up in the mornings. We both shared a passion for football, which of course, was another source of complaint against the school, as it was a rugby-playing school and we were fanatical supporters of Liverpool. George hated school even more than I did and our morning sessions would be spent on an exchange of views on the teachers that we hated the most. Top of the list was the headmaster, known simply as the 'Boss', a formidable personality who wanted to take this relatively new and predominantly working-class grammar school and inculcate the rituals and standards of an English public school. He was fiercely ambitious for the school and for its pupils, but these lofty ambitions were lost on George and I. He was tall with thinning grey hair which just covered a large domed head and his thick pebble glasses created an intimidating, wide-eyed, angry stare.

One of his pet hates was sloppy grammar and the Belfast idioms of speech and accent. As I had an accent as thick as buttermilk, I was in constant dread of coming into contact with him. But on one occasion, I was sent into an adjoining classroom to borrow some chairs and to my horror, I found him teaching a group of sixth formers.

'Sir, can I borrow some chairs?' As soon as I opened my mouth I felt my strong Belfast accent out there, out of its cage, circling the room for all to see, an easy victim for his ruthless mimicry.

'I don't know – can you?' he snapped. A tittering rose from the class in anticipation of some sport. I blushed furiously and looked confused. 'You look strong enough to lift a few chairs – well, can you?'

'Yes sir,' I stammered, missing the point.

'The correct grammar is MAY I. MAY I borrow some chairs.' He glared at me as if I'd committed some squalid act and dragged the reputation of the school into the gutter. I stumbled out of the class dragging a few chairs behind me, relieved that I got off so lightly.

One day George and I were rushing through the school gates. We were late and the playground was empty. We'd been kicking a stone to each other as we ran down the street, enacting, in our imagination, a brilliant display of inter-passing by Liverpool players in the final of the FA cup. On entering the playground George made one final kick at an imaginary set of goal posts, but unfortunately, I reacted instinctively and stuck out my right foot to intercept it. The stone ricocheted off my shoe and cracked the side window of the headmaster's car.

We stood frozen in horror looking at the window which now had a series of concentric cracks emanating from a small hole, rather as if a bullet had been fired at it.

'That was your fault – sticking your foot out,' George said, the survival instinct quickly surfacing as he sought to shift the blame.

'You kicked the stone – it came off my foot by accident,' I responded.

We guiltily looked around and could see no one in the playground but we couldn't be sure if the incident had not been seen from one of the school windows. We made our way quickly back into the school and spent the rest of the day in a high state of anxiety. What should we do? Make a clean breast of it or lie low, hoping that no one had seen us. We pondered the dilemma between classes, taking care that we were not overheard. The afternoon crawled by, interspersed with moments of heightened tension whenever we saw the headmaster in the corridor. That night I was physically sick with worry. Would I get expelled? I knew that my parents would be devastated as they were so proud of my success and I nearly broke down and told them.

The following morning, we waited anxiously for the start of the Assembly and the headmaster's opening remarks. We were not disappointed.

'Yesterday evening when I returned to my car, I found that the side window had been broken, probably by a stone being thrown at it. This could only have happened during school hours and almost certainly by a pupil at this school.' He paused dramatically and looked round at all our upturned faces. I felt that he was looking directly at me. 'Whilst I was not pleased to see the damage to my car,' he went on, 'I was very, very disappointed that the pupil concerned did not have the backbone to come to me and admit what he'd done.' There was a long pause. I wanted the ground to open up so that I could disappear. 'I now expect that pupil to do so.' He abruptly turned and ended the Assembly.

The following morning and for several mornings, he repeated the call for the culprit to own up, always accompanying his demand with an increasingly testily homily on moral courage and facing up to the implications of one's actions. George and I resolved never to speak about it to anyone; in any case we reckoned that any credit for an early guilty plea had long gone.

One morning many weeks later George confided to me

that his father was going to see the headmaster.

'What for?' I said, suddenly alarmed that it was connected to the accident.

'He's going to ask him if I can move schools.'

The next day George was gone and I never met him again. Life for me continued in its less than exciting projection, as I steadily moved up through the school and passed the requisite exams to become a prefect, a trusted member of the 'Boss's' praetorian guard. In the year after the infamous incident, our school moved its location to one of the leafy suburbs of Belfast, so we no longer had to run the daily gauntlet from the local jeering kids.

It was during my last year at school that I became aware of the new career that George was forging which grew by leaps and bounds to make him a household name throughout the land. I then followed his career avidly like everyone else and was proud of our brief friendship. Almost fifty years later, I watched his funeral ceremony being shown on television. The funeral hearse, snaking through the narrow streets lined with people on a damp grey morning and the elaborate and emotional ceremony, with many eulogies from family and friends. He had climbed to the peak of fame and fortune but had played out his life in the public eye, like a third-rate soap opera. But now George Best was dead and as I reflected back on my own life, I could not suppress the same rhetorical question, made famous from one of his anecdotal stories, where did it all go wrong?

* *the events depicted here are fictitious.*

THE WATCHMAN

It was the long summer of 1967 when pop music was worth listening to and girls in miniskirts, were certainly worth looking at. It was the year before the 'troubles' erupted in Belfast and civic society, which I had grown up with, would be changed forever. We lived in North Belfast in clear view of the Cave Hill on one side and the Divis Mountain on the other. All of our houses were tiny, semi-detached, two up and two down, with a tiny bathroom separating the two bedrooms. We were a staunchly Protestant street and very working class.

There was a whole crowd of interesting people that lived in our street: a family of gypsies who had forsaken the travelling life, a man who had done time for robbing a shop with a sawn-off shotgun, a 'strong man' who had reputedly hung from the carric-a-reed bridge by his teeth, another who was missing an ear. And then there were the Kanes. This was a family of twelve children and four racing greyhounds. They were not Catholic but as Mrs Kane once resignedly declared, 'Just stupid Prods.' All the children were boys except the last one; Maureen was the same age as me but, by the time she was born, the eldest three boys had emigrated to Australia! Her brother Trevor, who was next to her in age, was the black sheep of a family not known for its whiteness. He had spent a large slice of his adolescence in a remand school or as my mother called it, 'a school for bad boys'.

By contrast, I was a single child and, as my father had a steady job, we were relatively prosperous. Moreover, to the triumphant delight of my mother, I had secured a place at university and when I first left the house with my college scarf carelessly draped over my shoulders, my mother followed me to the gate, not just to watch my progress down the street but to see if auld McCartney was watching behind twitching curtains!

It is difficult to realise now, that in those days, Belfast seemed to be a place where nothing ever happened. Dullness hung over the city like the damp mist that would periodically descend on our street, softening the starkness of the deprivation. Boredom would be the order of the day and none more so that on the stern rectitude of an Ulster Sabbath. Here the place would resemble a ghost town where the selling of a cup of tea would be regarded as a dire violation! A famous photograph from the Irish Times showed the swings in a children's play area in a Protestant neighbourhood, heavily padlocked against use. The caption above the photograph declared that '*Catholics have more fun*', a humorous reference to the more relaxed attitude of the Catholic Church to Sunday activities.

How I dreaded the church services on a Sunday evening and the dreary sermon delivered by the minister who would pick some obscure tract from the Bible and build it into a theological dissertation of mind-numbing obtuseness. But I wouldn't be the only one who was suffering in silence. I remember looking round the congregation and seeing all the glazed eyes looking despondently at the bare altar, not one of them hearing his words, never mind listening to his sermon. They had too long been exposed to this weekly purgatory so that his words could no longer penetrate their devout deafness.

It would be my last year at college and troubling thoughts about where all this academic slog was taking me were starting to impinge upon my consciousness. But that was still a year away and as I sat on the old trolley bus with its silent acceleration and dirty windows, my main concern was getting off at the right stop. 'Look out for the BP garage and then get off immediately,' advised my father. Inevitably the bus had flashed past the garage and the stop before I had a chance to stir out of my seat. But I managed to scramble off at the next one and strolled back down the road.

It was the Shankill Road, one of the great tributaries out of the city centre, and a place that my mother declared 'was great for a wee bit of shappin!' The small shops, lining both sides of the road, provided the total range of household goods from TVs to crockery, from three-piece settees to clothes pegs and from butchers to fancy candle makers. The invisible hand of the marketplace ensured that everything on sale lay within the ambitions and budget of the acres of small terrace houses that lay behind. It was down one of these side streets that I had to find a small engineering firm, where I would be a 'day watchman' for the next two weeks when the firm closed for the holiday break.

It was an unremarkable and relatively small building from the front and initially I walked past it. It had two steel roller doors that were firmly closed and daubed with the inevitable *'No Pope here'* declaration to which some wag had scrawled below it, *'Lucky old Pope.'* I noticed a small alley way down the side and at the end of it there was a sturdy wooden door with peeling brown paint. I had been told to present myself in the factory by 9:00 a.m. and the existing 'watchman' would meet me. My new career owed itself to a recent change of legislation, which required two men to be on duty whenever a firm closed for the July fortnight.

I knocked on the door and waited, then knocked more loudly but nothing stirred. I looked at my watch. I was ten minutes early so I settled down on a small wall to wait. After fifty minutes I was ready to give up when an elderly man in shabby grey coat and baggy brown trousers, with a cloth cap pulled down over his forehead, came shuffling up the lane. He looked up, clearly startled, when I stood up and called out: 'Hello!'

'Who are youse?' he growled. Up closer I could see that he had a pronounced grey stubble, bright blue eyes that were bloodshot but still flashed a steady steely gaze in my direction.

'Hi. I'm waiting for a Mr. Molloy. I'm Billy Hawthorne...' I said but I could see my name meant nothing. 'I'm here to work as a watchman.'

He took off his cap and scratched his head. He still looked confused.

'Apparently, we need two watchmen to look after this place…' I said, hoping that there hadn't been a cock-up as the whole arrangement had been agreed at the last minute by my father who knew someone who knew someone…!!

'Ah, right. You're the st..st..student sent in to make sure I don't fa..fa..fa..fall asleep on the job.' He shot me a glance that was half amused but also had a hint of warning. What happened on his watch, he expected to stay on his watch.

He unlocked the door and pushed it open and I followed him along a narrow, scruffy corridor and then through another door, which opened out into a large workshop, packed full of engineering equipment. All the benches were positioned close together, with just enough room for a man to work and the benches themselves were loaded with an assortment of lathes, drilling machines, a large and fearsome-looking circular saw and gas welding equipment. It smelt of oil and dust.

It reminded me of the occasion when my father took me round his place of work, which was a large foundry dedicated to making linen machines. I was a weedy fifteen-year-old coming up to school leaving age and I remember being distinctly unimpressed by the noise, dirt and coldness of the factory floor and the rough banter of the men working there. 'Don't fret yourself over your exams, son. If you don't do well, I can get you in here on an apprenticeship.' Looking back, I'm sure that my father was employing a subtle form of motivation!

'We're in here,' he said, striding into a small office, which had a large desk in the corner and a couple of battered old armchairs against the wall. It also had a small sink and alongside stood an electric kettle with an assortment of chipped mugs.

'Time for a cu…cu…cuppa. My name's Pat,' he said as he filled the kettle. 'Named after the pa..pa..pa..patron saint of Ir..Ir..Ireland. And what about youse.? Were you na..na..named after King Bi..Bi..Billy?' His eyes twinkled as he spoke. He clearly wanted our different national identities to be acknowledged and out in the open.

'I hope not as my Uncle Willie will be very disappointed,' I replied, trying to enter into the same light hearted tone. This was a year before the 'troubles' exploded and consumed Northern Ireland's society in a bloody conflict for the next 30 years. There had been some bad-tempered rhetoric exchanged in the media between a firebrand, Protestant preacher and republican politicians, but that aside, normal societal relationships could be characterised as respectable, good mannered and eternally dull. Certainly, I had no issues with Pat Molloy, with either his religion or his allegiances, but I was certainly concerned that it could be a long two weeks to be stuck in a small office with an old guy with a stammer.

But how wrong it turned out to be! Pat was always late in the morning and was fairly uncommunicative until he had his cuppa. Then he would stand four-square at the table, legs slightly apart as if he was on a boat, cap firmly on his head, mug in his hand and he would start leafing through the morning newspaper. The paper was purchased for the horseracing tips but before he settled down to study them, he would regale me with a succinct commentary of the events of the previous day as reported in the paper and, in particular, the growing street unrest. As I got to know him and he became more relaxed in my company, the less pronounced was his stammer. It seemed to me that it encouraged a brevity of expression, a conciseness, where words superfluous to the overall meaning remained unsaid, and that any prolonged struggle over a particular word would, if anything, heightened the anticipation of the final declamation.

'Pais..Pais..Paisley is the sp..sp..spark that is go..going to set this place alight,' he declared one morning with remarkable foresight. I made some mumbling response. I was not interested in politics. Once I'd finished my course I was for the off, a prospect that both frightened and exhilarated me. It was time to leave the nest but to do what and where to go had yet to be resolved.

Pat's daily routine was simple and unvarying. After his perusal of the daily paper, he would take himself off to the bookies at the corner of the street, place his bets and then retire to the 'Wellington' situated next door, a particularly lucrative combination, where he would watch the races, drink steadily and enjoy the craic with his fellow punters. He would then make his way back to the factory around 3:00 p.m. and to the visible eye, no worse for drink. Instead for the next two hours, until we closed up, he would regale me with further stories from his life and times.

He was a roofer by trade and brought up a family of seven through repairing the roofs of the little terrace houses of his neighbourhood. It was a precarious living in every respect as he clambered over the slippery slate tiles, unencumbered by any safety legislation, and on more than one occasion, had lost his balance and was sliding down the roof when, 'by the Grace of God', his clothes got snagged or he managed to get his fingertips into some crack in the roof. These stories were naturally told in a halting manner but the necessary pauses only added to the sense of drama.

But what I enjoyed hearing about the most was the various ruses he had used to maximise a thin living. His most widely deployed one was when he was replacing broken slates; here, he would quietly move along the roofs of the terrace to a neighbouring property where he would calmly remove or dislodge the slates, thus ensuring repeat business. Sometimes he would add insult to injury by using the removed slates to repair the legitimate damaged ones! As the houses were all rented, he was able to placate his conscience, because those 'racketeering landlords' would have to pay. There was a twinkle in his eye when he told these stories of his less than honest endeavour, but I felt he was also closely observing my reaction as a potentially stiff-necked, censorious Protestant.

My own routine was even more straightforward. I was to inspect around the workshop first thing in the morning to ensure there had been no overnight break-in and then repeat the process last thing in the evening, checking that all windows were closed. There would be a number of workmen employed during the holiday fortnight, to carry out various maintenance activities, and I was to clock them in and keep 'an eye on them'. Exactly what the latter requirement entailed was never spelt out. However, it was academic as they turned out to be members of Pat's family and friends.

The three of them turned up late of the morning of my fourth day, after Pat had shuffled off up the road to seek his fortune with the 'gee-gees!' The informal leader of the group was Pat's son, Fergal, a young man in his middle twenties, of wiry build with black curly hair and blue eyes. He radiated friendliness and good humour and I liked him immediately. The taller of his companion was Neil, Fergal's cousin, a tall, lanky lad of the same age with a thin face, unruly black hair, and two large front teeth, which reminded one of a Disney character every time he smiled. And finally there was Brian, small and tubby with a face that still showed the ravages of acne, sandy-coloured hair which was in full retreat at the front and was combed forward without a parting to disguise the fact. He lived in the same street and was childhood friends with the other two, and while he was the least prepossessing physically, he made up for it by being the most vocal with an opinion on everything, which he was not reticent in sharing.

The maintenance work largely consisted of painting the workshop walls brown in order to better disguise the dirt and oil streaks which adorned them. The work was certainly not onerous and my merry little band went about it at a leisurely pace which allowed for generous tea breaks and lots of craic! The tea breaks were my responsibility, which I willingly insisted in taking on despite the democratic views of the group that it should be shared. I bought the tea and the milk and occasionally brought in some biscuits and scones. These breaks broke up the monotony of the day, and gave me an insight into a lifestyle and culture that was hidden from me behind the voluntary apartheid that existed in Belfast. Protestants and Catholics largely lived in their own areas, were educated separately and, in the main, did not socialise with one or other. Pat and his family and friends soon changed that for me.

'Da, do you remember when you abandon us in the Isle of Man?' It was during our afternoon cuppa and Fergal was gently teasing his father about a family incident in the past. Our tea breaks were dominated by storytelling, where a casual comment or a reference to some routine event, would trigger someone in the group to embark on a personal reminiscence, sometimes of doubtful veracity.

'You mean the t-t-ti..time that your m-m-m…mother and you failed to get on the boat,' Pat shot back, ready for the banter. Fergal, his mother and Pat had booked to go to the Isle of Man on a day trip, which meant catching an early sailing and then coming back on the last ferry at 5:00 p.m. It was agreed that Fergal, who was about ten years old at the time, and his mother would head for the beach and the funfair, while Pat would sample the local hospitality. Since it was well known that Pat's sense of time soon faded as the ambience of the pub took over, it was impressed upon him that Fergal and his mother would collect him, at the pub, in good time for the last sailing. Pat then proceeded to enjoy a very pleasant day, holding forth with a new group of drinking friends and becoming more befuddled with alcohol as the day wore on. Suddenly late afternoon his companions suddenly declared that they would have to leave as they too were catching the last ferry. Pat was immediately thrown into confusion as he could not remember exactly what was agreed; was he to make his own way to the boat or to remain in the pub to await his family? He was very aware that he had 'form' on these matters having missed the last train on a similar day excursion in the past.

'C'mon, Pat. She'll be on the boat waiting for ye.' His new best friends were urging him to join them so that they could resume their pleasant sojourn in the saloon bar on the boat. With some misgivings Pat went with them, thereby creating a story that had entered the annals of the family's folklore, and had clearly been re told many times. On discovering Pat's absence, Fergal and his mother desperately searched for him in the many bars up and down the main area of the town. Inevitably they ended up missing the boat themselves and had to spend a very long and uncomfortable night at the boat terminal. As for Pat, the realisation that his wife and son had been left behind didn't really dawn until the floor of the saloon bar started to lurch beneath his feet!

'I ne…ne…never did like the Isle of m..m..Man,' said Pat when the story was concluded with much merriment from me and, to a lesser extent, the rest of the group as they'd heard it before.

'Well we've never been back. That's for sure,' said Fergal, laughing.

On another occasion when we were sitting around at lunch time, Brian piped up and said, 'Do youse remember Humpy John?' There was a few unenthusiastic nodding of heads. They all knew what was coming. They'd all heard the story before but the unspoken etiquette on these occasions was to allow the storyteller free rein whenever there was an interested audience. And I was that audience! Humpy John was a 'poor wee soul' who had been born with the most dreadfully deformed spine which gave him a hump of epic proportions. 'When he was wearing his raincoat and you didn't know him, you would've thought he was carrying a bag of coal on his back,' said Brian. He'd lived his whole life in the same street and was well liked for his perpetual cheerfulness. 'Meeting Humpy always gave you a lift because he always had a joke to crack,' said Brian. After his mother died, Humpy lived on his own and became a fixture in the neighbourhood; as he got older, he was prone to anything that was "going round" but the community always looked out for him. Then one day a neighbour noticed a lack of activity in his house and a quick investigation revealed that Humpy had died in his sleep. A funeral was duly organised but then the undertaker, who was local and knew Humpy, came up with a problem. They couldn't close the lid of the coffin due to Humpy's hump! A crisis meeting of friends and neighbours was duly convened and various options discussed. The obvious one would've been to make the coffin deeper but that would mean a 'tailor made' coffin of exorbitant costs and delay. The solution finally agreed to would be to strap down Humpy's upper torso with a leather strap that wound its way round the bottom of the coffin and, secured by a metal buckle, would pull down poor old Humpy's chest until the lid could be fitted. The modification were duly made and pronounced a success so Humpy was laid out in his sitting room and his wake could truly start.

'And we gave Humpy a great send-off,' said Brian. 'Plenty of booze and music. The craic was spread over two nights and on the second night things were starting to flag. A group of women were sitting round the open coffin sipping their wee drinks, reminiscing about Humpy and what a poor life he'd led due to his hump. Auld Minnie Taylor, who has a tongue like a viper, said it was a great pity that he didn't marry as he would have made a lovely wee husband. Then Big Bertha said that, just before he died, Humpy had told her about what'd happened between him and Sadie Crothers. That certainly got everyone's attention,' chortled Brian, recalling the incident. 'Sadie Crothers was a vinegarish old spinster known for her devout ways,' said Brian by way of explanation. 'Anyway, Big Bertha said that she'd been sworn to secrecy but now that he was dead she supposed it didn't matter now. And she was leaning forward about to spill the beans when…' Brian paused to heighten the moment of drama, 'the buckle on the strap slipped and Humpy's head suddenly popped up above the level of the coffin!!' We all fell about laughing, even those who'd heard it before, and Brian sat back, pleased about his rendition of a story that must have been told many times. 'And to this day Big Bertha has refused to say what'd happened between Humpy and Sadie Crothers,' added Brian to renewed laughter.

And so, the days merged seamlessly into each other, all following the same leisurely pattern. I was conscious that as a university student, I was regarded as something of a rare species, occupying an elevated position in their minds of being something of 'a brain box'. Almost shyly they asked me what I was studying and when I said Law, I was immediately inundated with questions ranging from their consumer rights over a motor bike, bought in good faith, but which turned out to be stolen; the authority of the police in searching people's houses; the likely success of their Aunt Josephine's challenge on her mother's will, and so on. For most of their queries, at best, I could only mumble something about a legal principle or a case precedent that might impact on the issue they were concerned about. I felt embarrassed and a little humble at how they would solemnly listen to my superficial judgements and it suddenly brought home to me how the whole edifice of the law impinged on the life of ordinary people.

One morning they all trooped in carrying various musical instruments and a large bag from which there was the unmistakable clink of bottles. It was Pat's birthday and we were going to have a party. I was unaware of the impending event and was a little put out that I had nothing to contribute but Fergal assured me to relax and just enjoy the show. First instrument out of its case and handled with loving care by Pat was the Irish pipes or more correctly known as the uilleann pipes. Initial impression was that they were the same as the

Scottish bagpipes but then I watched Pat as he strapped the bellows to his waist and started to inflate the bag by pumping his arms. He looked up at me with a twinkle in his eye.

'You see my mouth will be free,' he said, a clear reference to the difference with the Scottish pipes that I was more familiar with. 'So, you'll be able to hear my lovely tenor tones.'

Fergal in the meantime was unpacking his fiddle, Neil a small circular drum which I later learnt was called a bodhran and Brian produced a tin whistle from his inside pocket. All of them set about tuning their instruments with commendable concentration despite the cacophony of competing sounds.

'We'll start with St. Bridgit's Day,' said Pat as they all sat round in a semi-circle with opened bottles of beer readily at hand. For the next couple of hours, I was treated to a most wonderful medley of sounds and tunes, all played from memory as there was not a music score to be seen. At various times a particular instrument would take centre stage and the other players would wait with concentrated stillness until it was their cue to re-join the group. The unique sound and particular skill of each instrument and its player was individually singled out and celebrated and I was truly smitten. Even Brian and his tin whistle produced a sound of such haunting quality that it lingered in my mind for days after.

At the end of the recital, I mumbled my appreciation, which sounded inadequate and feeble, perhaps due to an innate Protestant reticence to show too much enthusiasm for republican culture. But what I could not deny was my astonishment that this group of working men, who existed in the precarious world of casual employment, could display such a rich hinterland. They had no trade but were willing to have a go at most tasks given the opportunity; they had limited future prospects and were often patronised, looked down upon as people of little consequence. And yet here they were articulate, thoughtful and with a sharp wit capable of ridiculing the institutions and politicians responsible for the inequalities that they laboured under.

It was late the following afternoon when I heard the rapping on the front door. I was sitting reading; Pat had long departed to seek his fortune and the gang were hard at work painting the walls. The knocking had been partially muffled by an internal door but when I opened that door, I was very conscious of the furious knocking and indeed kicking of the outside door. I flung the door opened and was greeted by three young men of about my own age who were grouped together on the front step. All were dressed in ill-fitting T-shirts, jeans and an assortment of jackets. They all looked at me with undisguised aggression. The taller and probably the oldest of the group took a step towards me so that his face was only inches away from mine. He locked a pair of hard blue eyes onto mine. I noticed a short scar on his cheek.

'Yes,' I said, conscious of the slight quiver in my voice.

'It's been reported that Popeish music was being played here yesterday afternoon.'

'Popeish music. What do you mean?' I was genuinely puzzled.

'You know Irish music. De-ye-ah-de-de-yah-de-de,' he said in mock imitation of an Irish jig. One of his friends sniggered. I thought quickly. There had been isolated spates of street violence in recent days over the flying of the tricolour flag in republican political offices and now was clearly not the time or place to admit to any displays of Irish culture.

'Nah,' I said trying to sound unfazed. 'The only music here is from a transistor radio that we've on.'

'My friend said he heard it clearly and it was unmistakably Irish music with the fiddles and the pipes.' The hard man edged his face even closer to mine but I held my ground and returned his stare.

'And I'm saying the only music here is from the radio. The reception in here is diabolical so we're always fiddling to get a station. Maybe we picked up some Irish music.' They say that the best ideas spring to mind when under pressure and my little porky caused them to pause.

'Where are youse from?' The hard man was now changing tact. I gave him the name of our street safe in the knowledge that its loyalist credentials were impeccable.

'Did youse know Trevor Kane?' the smallest member of the group asked.

'I should do so since he lives four doors up. And I know his sister Maureen too,' I added as a way of further confirming the local connection.

'She's a slag,' the hard man said with a sneer.

'I'll let Trevor know of your opinion,' I replied evenly and had the satisfaction of seeing a flicker of alarm in his eyes.

'Who else is in there?' he asked, nodding his head in the direction of the workshop.

'Only a couple of lads doin' a bit of painting,' I replied.

'Well tell 'em to keep their transistor tuned in to good Prod music,' he said, giving me a last intimidatory stare.

'I'll pass it on,' I replied, staring evenly back. But I knew his last comment was aimed at allowing him to withdraw without loss of face. He turned round and all of them were about to walk back down the alleyway when Pat suddenly appeared. He had his cap pulled down over his eyes and there was a faint hint of unsteadiness in his gait. My heart sank. I could not believe in the timing, a few minutes later they would have missed each other. I'd worked hard to keep the two sides apart but now a collision was inevitable.

'Hi, Pat. How's those auld nags behaving?'

Pat stopped in his tracks and looked up.

'Well, well!! If it's not Ch..Ch…Charlie's son. You're in for a tr..tr…treat tonight, my boy. Your da r..r…rode an incredible run of luck this afternoon. Four s..s..straight wins, one after the other. It's going to be ch..ch..chips and caviar for you and your mother tonight. Or at least it would be if you could buy caviar in this go…go…godforsaken hole.'

I could not believe my ears! Instead of a major confrontation, a re-run of the Battle of the Boyne, Pat was engaged in friendly bantering conversation with all of them but particularly my erstwhile opponent, the hard man, who I now learnt was called Jack. Despite the good humour, now clearly on display, I was anxious to drag Pat away in case he inadvertently reopened the issue by asking Jack the obvious question of why was he here!

'Pat. Fergal needs your help. I think its urgent,' I said in desperation.

Pat was reluctant to move as he was in the middle of describing each race and the bookies odds that the eventual winner was given.

'I'm tellin' ye, that auld bookie, f..f..foxy f..f..face, was lookin pig s..s..sick by the end,' Pat told his delighted audience. 'I made it wo..wo..worse for him by backing the same wi..wi..winner in the last race.'

Eventually the group moved off and I was able to shepherd Pat back inside.

'How do ye know that crowd of hard wee loyalists?' I could not avoid asking.

'I've known Ch..Ch..Charlie Knox for years and Wee Jack and his b..b..brothers used to play with mine when we met up on a St..St..Saturday afternoon.'

I then told Pat what had happened and how I persuaded them the music must have come from the transistor. As I was relating it, I realised that my action must have sounded cowardly in Pat's ears; that I'd allowed myself to be intimidated by a small group of thugs into denying one of the bulwarks of their cultural identity. But Pat sat for a few minutes in silence with his head bowed and when he spoke the sadness in his voice was unmistakable.

'Goddamn the po..po..politicians in this sh..sh..shite hole. They kn..kn..know the bu..bu..buttons to p..p..press and when they do we d..d..dutifully respond. Last October I was talking to Ch..Ch..Charlie about a joint con..con..concert with my group and his flute band sh..sh..sharing the musical score. We'd play each other's p..p..party songs.' Pat sighed and then looked up at me. 'This p..p..place will never ch..ch..change until we get to know each other and enjoy each other's cu..cu..culture.' Those words still echo with me fifty years later. Alas, little has changed.

A few days later we all packed up to go. Our two-week stint had come to an end and on Monday the workforce would be back and the place would be humming with the noise of machinery and the ribald banter of the workmen. I was sad to see it finish. Contrary to my initial expectation I had greatly enjoyed the company of Pat and his little family group. The leisurely breaks were filled with good conversation, anecdotal stories and lots of laughter and I admired the rich cultural hinterland that they had shared with me.

While I was packing away my last few bits and pieces into my rucksack, I saw Fergal approach me from the side of my eye.

'Billy,' he said. 'We'd like to give you this small gift as a thank-you for being the best tea boy we ever had.'

'And the b..b..best educated,' said Pat to laughter all round.

Fergal thrust a mug into my hand which had some Irish inscribed on it. I was completely taken aback, embarrassed and humbled in equal measure.

'You shouldn't have done that,' I stammered. 'It was nothing and I enjoyed your company.'

'Look what the mug says,' said Pat. ' Ni dearc go cur le cheile,' he said fluently and without a trace of a stammer. 'Or in En..En..English… There is no strength without unity.'

I never saw any of them again. But I've still got the mug.

THE IRISH HOLIDAY

John Buchan had once written about his favourite place in Scotland that it was a place *'a man might set out from, and to which he might return when he had fought his battles, but in which he dared not pitch his camp till he had won the right to rest'*. It was forty years ago when I last set foot in the holiday resort of my youth and I was now returning with a car load of my own children, all of whom would much rather be returning to last year's holiday villa in Majorca.

'Is it much further?' asked my son.

I glanced at him through the rear-view mirror, wedged between his two elder sisters, disconsolately playing with his iPad. It had been a long tiring journey by car, up through the length of England, on the endlessly boring M6 motorway and then across the interminable and winding A75 road towards the little town of Stranraer and the Irish ferry. We were now on the equally twisting coastal road heading for the northerly tip of Northern Ireland.

'We're almost there,' I replied, peering at the rainswept road ahead and praying that the weather would not be like this all week. How different it was when I was my son's age. In those days the week's holiday in Portrush, on the Causeway Coastline, was looked forward to with an intensity that surpassed even that other important date in my calendar, Christmas.

Simple pleasures were the order of the day in those days. My mother would pack and re-pack two battered old suitcases which had to be wrestled down from the loft. Every year my father would crack the same joke that we were only going for a week and not permanently emigrating. Cars were a rarity in our neighbourhood so the journey was taken by steam train, on seats that had to be booked weeks in advance. Making the seat reservations signalled the start of the countdown for the holiday and my father would further sharpen my sense of expectancy by taking me on the platform to view 'our train'. No wonder steam trains retain their special affection down the years and I can still remember my sense of awe on looking at this huge black iron monster which, even in repose, would let out gasps of steam and pulsate with a life of its own.

To this day I can still recount the stations en route almost like a mantra – Antrim, Ballymena, Ballymoney, Coleraine, Portstewart and finally Portrush. When you are 10 years old, the journey seems like eternity, especially coped up in the old-style carriages which had no corridor and a ventilation system which relied on gingerly lowering the carriage door window with a leather strap which resembled that used by barbers for sharpening their cutthroat razors. The twists and turns of the track ahead, along with the swirling coastal breeze, would ensure that bracing fresh air was soon replaced with smoke and there would be a rush to pull the window back up.

At long last the train would make its final approaches to

Portrush Station and the struggle with the window would be cheerfully abandoned. I would lean out as far as I could to catch a glimpse of that point where the sky began to drop, revealing at first the wind-white sea, then the rocky coves and finally the golden curve of the west strand and the small harbour with its cluster of bathing boxes.

The girl at reception wore a neat red jacket with a silk blue scarf fastened with a large pearl broach at her throat.

'I will get someone to take your suitcases up to your room, sir,' she said in the soft brogue which owed much to its Scottish ancestry.

'Do the children know about our games room?' she asked sympathetically, looking at my children as they stood in a bored huddle at the reception desk. 'We have a billiards table, a skittles alley and loads of computer games and we have an indoor swimming pool,' she added, trying to inject some excitement into her recital of the facilities.

'The kids will certainly like the pool, especially in this weather,' my wife replied in a tone that made it quite clear that this year's holiday was my idea alone. Outside, across the hotel's car park, I could see the flags of different nationalities flapping heavily in the Atlantic breeze and beyond that the sea and sky were joined in a seamless slate grey canopy.

'The weather can only get better,' I said, more in hope than conviction.

It was all very different at Mrs Boyd's guest house forty years ago. We always got the room right at the top of the house which had a long sloping ceiling over my parents' double bed and which caused a few bumped heads and much mirth until they learnt to duck at the right moment. It also had a small window fitted into the roof, from which by standing on my tip toes, I could see across half the town to the rolling sand hills of the magnificent east strand, one of the longest beaches in Ireland.

Three meals a day were served at precise times, each meal heralded by a vigorous thumping of a metal gong, which would be the signal for everyone to emerge from their rooms, where they had been waiting with quiet anticipation, and make their way in an unhurried but purposeful manner to the dining room. This regimented system, which offered no flexibility to personal plans or tastes, was never resented by anyone, but instead widely marvelled by all the women guests who frequently remarked that 'they didn't know how Mrs Boyd coped!'

Our hotel was some mile and a half from Portrush town along the coastal road which linked it with its sister town of Portstewart. Everyone was tired, irritable and hungry from the journey.

'I noticed a restaurant directly opposite. It looks interesting. Shall we go there?' I asked with a forced cheerfulness. My wife gave me a look, which clearly indicated that I was still a long way off from redeeming myself.

The restaurant turned out to be a great success despite its contrived name of 'Some Other Plaice'. It was small and homely and in spite of the fact that it was August, had a welcoming coal fire burning in the main dining room. It was perched looking out to sea and on a clear night we would have been treated to a spectacular sunset. Instead the rain lashed against the windows in sudden squally bursts and the fading evening light added to the general wintry gloom. The restaurant was run by a young French couple who had fallen in love with this part of Ireland and it was amusing to listen to their talk, which was liberally sprinkled with Ulster idioms of speech, but still retained a distinctive French accent. I was in a much more relaxed and expansive mood as we made our way back across to the hotel. I could not help thinking that if a French couple decided to settle here then it couldn't be such a bad place and that I should stop feeling guilty about imposing my nostalgic whim on the family.

'I'm looking forward to start exploring tomorrow,' I said.

One year I met a young lad of the same age staying at Mrs. Boyd's guest house. His name was Sean and he was a big-boned, slow-of-speech, ginger-headed country boy whose parents owned a small farm about 50 miles from the coast. By comparison, he made me feel quick witted, slick, street wise and (unbelievable to say) sophisticated. But that was not the only difference between us. He was a Catholic and I was from staunchly Protestant stock. At school we had dinned into us over and over again the Protestant story and how it had triumphed against the unrelieved darkness of Rome. Portrush was also a Protestant town and many gable walls declared the legend 'No Pope here' and even ruder slogans against His Holiness. Despite these entrenched cultural barriers, we hit it off immediately and were soon planning our rendezvous for the following day.

He was an easy companion to be with, happy to defer to my superior knowledge of the town and go along with my suggestions. We would discuss life at school, the subjects we liked, the teachers we hated but it was only when we touched upon sport that we became conscious of our different backgrounds. He played Irish hurling whilst I played rugby and our discussion would centre around a none-too-subtle game of one-upmanship, in which we tried to score points of each other on what game was the hardest with tales of injuries received. However, it was his stories of life on the farm that had me stumped, for there was nothing comparable I could counter them with. I was secretly impressed at the amount of hard physical work that he had to fit in around his school day, from the early-morning chores of feeding the chickens and milking the cows, to the harvesting of the hay in the late summer evenings. In fact, this was the first holiday that he and his parents ever had and that was only brought about because the family doctor recommended some sea air to 'help his chest'. All of this was related in his soft country accent and in an unobtrusive, modest manner, which blunted any instinctive desire on my part to counter score.

We would get together at the end of each meal and have unfettered freedom to do what we liked; my parents were delighted that I had found a 'chum to play with' instead of moping about with them, as a typically moody early teenager. Sean's parents, who seemed much older than my own parents, appeared to be equally content, although they also appeared to be ill at ease in Mrs Boyd's dining room and did not enter into any of the casual conversations that went on between the tables. Sean's father was a strongly built man whose long, lugubrious, red face bore witness to a job in the outdoors in all weathers. But what made him really stand out was that he wore a charcoal suit, with a waistcoat and tie and immaculately polished black boots, which laced up to his ankles, on every single day of the holiday. My mother, of course, identified the reason immediately, his wardrobe clearly must consist of either his daily farm working clothes or his 'Sunday best' and clearly this holiday, in a seaside guest house, warranted only his best. His wife was similarly sartorially challenged. She was a small, dark-haired woman who had her hair tied up into an old-fashioned bun at the back and always wore the same black dress, relieved only by a single strand of white pearls around her neck. And there they sat every meal time, like a couple attending a funeral, self-contained and silent, munching their way diligently through everything that was put in front of them. I noticed that Sean too hardly ever spoke at the table but instead kept his head down and concentrated on his food.

There is always the danger that nostalgia has distorted the memory but my recollection of that summer holiday was of glorious summer days when the two of us explored every nook and cranny of the town; from the emptiness at the end of the east strand where the chalk white rocks hung over the beach and the gulls wheeled and screeched overhead in defence of their nests, to the small putting course with its treacherous lumps and bumps which conspired to alter the direction of a golf ball when its trajectory seemed certain. We even managed to chat up a couple of local girls that we met at the amusement arcadia. They were hanging about the juke box and started to badger us to choose an Elvis Presley song when we sauntered up to make a selection. They were both born and bred in Portrush and their strong country accent was sometimes incomprehensible to my ears but gave me a widely inflated sense of my own worldliness and I proceeded to bombard them with exaggerated stories of my life in Belfast. However, I soon noticed, with a sharp stab of chagrin, that despite my scintillating discourse the prettier of the two had only eyes for Sean who all this time had been standing sheepishly beside me and contributing little to the chat up.

On the penultimate day of our holidays when a sense of gloom was settling on our spirits, I suggested that we go to the open-air swimming pool.

'I'll have to ask me maw,' said Sean.

'Why?' I asked. 'It's not far.'

'She doesn't like me goin' near water,' he replied.

He came back some minutes later with his trunks wrapped in a towel but with a worried look on his face.

'They have gone out for a walk. I suppose it'll be all right.'

'Sure it will,' I reassured him. 'It's goin' to be freezing. We'll not stay long.'

The swimming pool was really a rock pool that had a series of ragged black rocks enclosing it against the sea on one side and a rough man-made wall completing the enclosure on the other side. The water in the pool was continually refreshed by sea water which came rushing through the various crooks and crannies with each surge of the tide. There were only a few hardy souls already in the pool as we braced ourselves for an icy encounter with sea water which last touched land in Northern Canada. I had brought a ball with me and once I had regained something resembling my normal breathing pattern, I started to knock it back and forth with Sean. But it soon became very apparent that Sean was struggling. His face was very pale and he seemed to have trouble breathing. Suddenly he turned and started to scramble out of the pool.

'Come on, you big Jinny…' but before I could remonstrate further, Sean collapsed by the side with his mouth wide open and his whole body convulsing as if he could not get air into his lungs. I was rooted to the spot, horrified and uncomprehending about what was happening.

The rest all happened in a blur of activity. A small crowd soon gathered round Sean. I saw a lady giving mouth-to-mouth resuscitation; an ambulance arrived followed by a police car and I was helped to dress before being taken in the police car back to the guest house. I felt sure that Sean had died and I was sobbing uncontrollably by the time I was delivered into the arms of my parents. I can remember clearly my mother's anxious face as she rocked me gently in her arms. Sean's parents had already been informed by the police and taken directly to the hospital.

Sometime later I was lying in bed, emotionally exhausted and drifting off to sleep when my mother shook my shoulder.

'Look who's here,' she said.

I looked up from my bed to see Sean standing there with a rather sheepish grin on his face. I could hardly believe it and although we had been friends for only a short period, I had felt responsible for what had happened.

'You can talk to him in the morning,' said my mother. 'There has been enough excitement for one day.'

But I never did speak to him again as Sean and his parents left before breakfast. As my mother described them, Sean's parents 'kept themselves to themselves' and offered no explanation about what had happened but the general consensus among the guests at the breakfast table was that Sean had suffered a 'fit'.

'How about a last stroll round the town?' I enquired hopefully.

'No chance,' replied my eldest daughter without taking her eyes off the TV.

The rest of the family did not bother to respond but their unwavering attention to the television screen made it clear that their answer would be the same. It was the last morning of our holidays and my wife was busy packing up in the bedroom. The holiday was hardly a success; the weather had stubbornly remained dismal and although we explored all the points of interest along that dazzling coastline, venturing further and seeing more than I ever did on all the summer holidays with my parents, it did not engage the present generation, brought up on a rich fare of Mediterranean sunshine, water skiing, scuba diving and lounging by an open-air swimming pool.

I made my way down into town for a final visit. I felt that it was unlikely that I would ever return and I wanted to commit to memory the sounds, the smells, the tangy taste of salt in the air, the sight of the Arcadia ballroom perched on the small rocky headland and all the small shops selling their cheap holiday souvenirs. I could not help reflecting on how little had changed; it was almost like entering a time warp with every street and corner invoking memories of the past. I wondered about Sean. Did he become a farmer like his father? The 'troubles' were particularly vicious in the area around his farm and I wondered if he had he been sucked into joining the republican paramilitaries. If I met him today perhaps, I wouldn't recognise the easy going, good-natured friend from my childhood. I had to admit that I'd changed too. I was no longer the child whose life had been confined to the dreary backdrop of a working-class housing estate. I was now a middle class, middle-aged man who had a lifetime of different experiences to draw upon. In all honesty I had to admit that the town was smaller and shabbier than the golden memory I'd harboured over the years. Rising prosperity and changing tastes had seen families moving further afield for their holidays and Portrush had gradually declined into catering for the day-tripper.

And yet… and yet… the magic had not entirely faded. As I stood looking across to the rolling sand dunes of my youth, I could still fleetingly recapture that surge of intense excitement, when I first stepped off the train and the whole holiday was before me. I've never since heard a seagull's cry without being momentarily transposed to that little harbour and the small fishing trawler landing its catch; all subsequent beaches have been unconsciously compared with the magnificent east strand and all have been found wanting.

As I turned back to the hotel and to my present life and family in a different country and decade, I wondered if Buchan was not right, that everyone should have a place to return to when all is said and done.

ABOUT THE AUTHOR

Mark Baird is a retired IT Director who acquired a postgraduate degree in computer science in 1968 and then went on to have a distinguished career in informatics in the NHS.

He has been a magistrate, a governor at a Further Education College and a non-executive director at a Local Health Board.

Mark lives with his wife Adela in Cardiff, Wales. They have three children and six grandchildren.